Spawn & Spitfire

Satan's Spawn MC Series

#1

K.J. Dahlen

Credits

KJ Dahlen Books
Spawn & Spitfire
Satan's Spawn MC Series
Copyright ©, 2018
Editor: Leanore Elliott
Book Design & Formatting: Wicked Muse[1]
Cover Art Provided By: Book Cover Love

---

1. https://www.facebook.com/WickedLeanore/

Description
Spawn & Spitfire
Satan's Spawn MC Series
#1

When Cassie comes to Troy, New York, looking for her best friend Peaches, she meets Deke Tory and her world is never going to be the same. He is formidable, magnetic and not like anyone she has ever met. Deke is president of the Satan's Spawn MC and while he lives by a certain set of rules, Cassie grew up differently. She grew up on the streets from the age of ten and the only rule there...was the rule of survival.

Deke finds himself drawn to the Spitfire girl who appeared out of nowhere. Can he break down the walls she has built up to protect herself? When Cassie and Peaches are reunited, their past comes back to haunt them. Someone from their past wants them dead to hide a terrible secret.

Can Deke protect her—can he even hold on to her?

They have to find a way to survive and Cassie has to find a way to keep a promise she made to her friend, Peaches, when they were ten. She has to find Peaches' family and reunite them. Will they both survive long enough or will their past swallow them?

Dedication

I would like to dedicate this book to all those women and children who have been caught up in desperate situations. I may not know your pain but I hope you are able to find a place like Redemption House to rebuild your lives. You have the strength deep down inside you to take that first step. I pray that you can find it within yourself to take that step and better your life.

CHAPTER ONE

When she walked into the Dirty Dancing club, Cassie didn't really know what she would find. The place was clean at least. As she looked around, she could see the bar and tables. She could also see the stage and the runway area. All she knew for sure was she needed to find her.

Smoke filled the room with its hazy scent and she wrinkled her nose a bit. Making her way through the tables to the bar, Cassie sat down and ordered a drink. When the bartender placed the glass in front of her, she turned slightly and watched the dancers for a moment. She grabbed the glass, brought it to her lips and asked, "Do you have a dancer here named Peaches?"

The bartender, a big man with tattoos up and down his arms narrowed his eyes at her question, then shrugged. "I'm here to serve drinks, not to answer dumb questions."

Cassie narrowed her own eyes then taking her drink, she began to wander around the club. She watched everything without seeming to notice anything. Slowly making her way toward the back hall, she saw one of the dancers enter the Ladies room. Placing her glass on the table, she headed that way herself. Pushing open the door, she saw the dancer checking her makeup. "Hi." She nodded at the dancer.

"Hey." The dancer nodded back.

"I was wondering if you could help me."

The dancer stopped what she was doing and stared at her through the mirror. "Whatcha looking for?"

Cassie held up her hands. "I just need some information on one of your dancers."

The woman frowned. "Sorry no can do, sister. We don't give out info on each other. We protect ourselves and the club."

"I can relate to that. I'm not asking for anything but if you have a dancer here named Peaches. I really need to find her. To make sure she's okay. I'm not here to hurt anyone, but I do need to find her."

"Sorry honey can't help you, club rules." The dancer moved toward the door.

Cassie moved aside to let her pass. "She's my friend and I need to know she's all right," she whispered. "I swear, that's all I want to know."

The woman paused. "If Deke finds out I told you anything, I'll be in so much trouble."

Cassie shook her head. "He won't find out from me. If you see her, tell her to call me at the Star Bright motel, room 104. Just get the message to her. Nobody has to know we even spoke. Please?"

The dancer nodded then left and the door closed slowly behind her.

For the first time since this nightmare began, Cassie let a deep hopeful breath.

A few minutes later, she walked out of the rest room and to the main door of the dance hall.

~****~

She didn't see the three men that followed her to the parking lot and watched as she got into her jeep and drove away.

One of the men lit a cigarette and as the smoke cleared, he said, "Deke might want to know about this." He turned and walked back into the club. As he made his way to the back room where the offices were, he nodded to the bartender.

At the big oak door of Deke's office, the man paused briefly and knocked. When Deke called out, he opened the door and came inside. The office was neat and tidy. The large oak desk in front of him was littered with papers and a laptop but he paid them no mind. As his eyes met the man's gaze behind the desk, Wiley swallowed hard.

Deke was a big man, six foot six inches, and at least three hundred fifty pounds of raw muscle. His short black hair was brushed back away from his face and his eyes were the color of ice. His hands were just as big as the rest of him and could easily break a man in half. "What's up, Wiley?"

"We have someone sniffing around, asking questions about one of the dancers."

Deke sat back in his chair. His fingers steepled while his steely gaze met his Sergeant at Arms. "Now who would be foolish enough to do that?"

Wiley shrugged. "It was a young woman. She first asked Hal about her but when Hal wouldn't give her any answers, she went into the ladies room after Candy. I don't think Candy would talk, but you never know what chicks are gonna say."

"Bring Candy in here," Deke ordered as he got up and moved from behind his desk.

A few minutes later, Wiley escorted Candy into the office.

She took one look at the big man's face and began to tremble.

"I understand we had someone asking about Peaches."

Candy groaned. "She asked but I didn't answer."

"What did she want to know?"

"She said she was a friend and just wanted to know if Peaches was okay," Candy answered truthfully. "She told me to have Peaches call her."

"Call her where?"

"She's at the Star Bright, room 104. I swear boss that's all she said."

Deke stared at the woman for a moment then nodded. "It's okay, you aren't in trouble, but the next time someone asks anything, you better be the one to bring it to my attention, not Hal or Wiley. I run a good place here and give you girls the protection you need to feel safe. I need you to look out for each other as well."

Candy almost wilted in relief. "I understand boss. I'm sorry I didn't come to you first thing."

Deke watched as she turned and left. Then he looked over at Wiley. "Maybe you and a couple of the boys should go find this woman and bring her to me. I need to know what she wants with Peaches."

"Sure thing Prez." Wiley grinned as he turned to leave.

"Don't hurt her man," Deke called out, "Just bring her in."

Wiley nodded at two other men and they all made their way to the parking lot. Mounting their bikes, they roared off.

A few minutes later, they parked near the Star Bright Motel, just down a few spots from the Jeep he'd seen the woman drive away in. Wiley glanced around the parking lot. No one else was around and he didn't want trouble.

Dismounting their rides, they all made their way to the door of room 104. He knocked and waited for an answer. When it didn't come right away, he pounded on the door.

A moment later, it was thrown open and a young girl stood there. "What the hell do you want?" she growled.

Wiley took a moment to look at her.

Dressed in a white motel robe she was a small woman, her long, red, wet hair fell to her waist in tiny ringlets. Her green eyes snapped with impatience.

Wiley was both impressed and puzzled with the fact that she didn't seem to fear them. "The boss wants to see you."

She crossed her arms over her chest and tapped her foot. "Well maybe, I don't want to see *your* boss. Did you ever think about that?"

Wiley's brow rose as he stared at her in astonishment. "When Deke says come lady, you come." He reached out to grab her.

She backed a step away. "I'm warning you, I don't like to be touched. And this Deke joker can go fuck himself. Who the hell does he think he is?"

Wiley growled and stepped forward to grab hold of her. "He's the fucking President of the Satan's Spawn MC, that's who the fuck he is!"

"I told you I don't like to be touched." She seethed as she took another step back.

"I don't really give a shit what you like or don't like. You're coming with us."

As soon as he grabbed her arm, she went postal. Her knee met his groin and before he even fell, she roundhoused his jaw and laid him out on the floor.

The other two men with him were stunned for a moment then charged at her.

She kicked one of them in the stomach and grabbed the other by his balls. Squeezing them viciously, she dropped him to the floor while giving the first one a hit to the eye.

He dropped beside Wiley and all three men laid there while they groaned.

She stepped away and headed for the bathroom. Closing the door, she got dressed and a couple of minutes later, rejoined the three men.

They were just starting to pick themselves up from the floor.

"I warned you not to touch me." She moved over to the bed, picked up her purse, and stood at the door. "Let's go see this boss man of yours. I have some questions I need answers to and since he's THE PRESIDENT," she emphasized the words with sarcasm in her voice. "He should have all the answers I need."

Wiley ran his hand along his jaw and felt the bruise she'd given him. His eyes sparkled with fury. "You're riding with one of us."

"Like hell I am," she snapped as she made her way out the door. "I have my own vehicle and I'll meet you there." She walked over to her jeep and got inside.

Wiley and the others got on their bikes and revved the engines. When they tore out of the parking lot, she followed them back to the club. They were waiting for her to get out of her jeep and then they followed her inside.

Hal, the bartender gaped at them.

Wiley and Jared had bruises on their faces and Jack was holding his belly. Jack and Jared made their limping, groaning way to the bar while Wiley motioned for her to go down the hall to the back of the club.

Two other men fell in behind her but they were far enough behind her to not bother her much it seemed.

Wiley knocked on the door and when Deke called out, Wiley opened it and motioned for her to go inside.

Deke glanced up at his man and looked stunned to see the bruises on his face. "What the fuck happened to you?"

Wiley raised his eyebrow and motioned toward the woman standing next to him.

Deke turned and appeared to be surprised to see her glaring back at him.

"You know, if you want someone's attention, it behooves you to be polite about it. Instead of ordering your muscle men to fetch me, you could have asked nicely."

~ * * * *~

Deke was shocked. He couldn't for the life of him find the words he wanted to blast her with. His men looked just as stunned as they gasped at her statement. "Do you have any idea who I am?" he finally growled.

She shrugged her shoulders. "Of course I know who you are. Do you think I'm stupid? You're the great big boss man of the Satan's Spawn, Deke Tory."

Jack and Jared joined them and Deke could see both men were in pain. Jared was holding his stomach while Jack was holding an ice bag to his balls. He glanced over at the little slip of a girl and noted she didn't seem to have any bruises on her at all.

Standing proud with her shoulders back and at all of five feet nothing, her red hair flowed down her back and her bright green eyes observed him carefully. Her arms were crossed over her ample chest and she couldn't weigh more than a hundred and 10 soaking wet.

"Who the hell are you anyway?" he finally asked.

She shook her head. "My name isn't important, my mission here is."

"And what would that mission be?" Deke asked.

"I'm here looking for a dancer named Peaches. All I want to know is if she's okay. I'm not looking for trouble of any kind, I just want to find her." She paused and stared at the big man behind the desk. "Why is that so difficult for you jackasses to figure out?"

Deke felt a streak of rage go through him. "This jackass protects his dancers and when someone he doesn't know starts asking questions, he wants to know why."

She dropped her arms and took a few steps toward his desk. Placing her fingers on the wooden surface, she leaned toward him. "Do you know Peaches?' she asked him softly. She gazed unto his eyes.

"Yes, I know Peaches," Deke finally told her.

"Is she okay?"

He frowned at her question. "Yes, she's okay. Why would you ask me that?"

She stood away from the desk. "I just wanted to find her and talk to her. I didn't mean any trouble. Will you have her call me? I need to speak to her."

"What the hell did you do to my men?" Deke asked softly.

His men shifted nervously. They knew when he spoke in that tone of voice he was in a fine rage. They knew to steer clear of him at that point. They almost felt sorry for her, almost. And Wiley thought she would soon see his temper, he grinned.

"I warned them that I don't like to be touched. They didn't listen." She shrugged. "Maybe now they will."

~****~

Deke stood to his impressive height and she could finally see just how big a guy he really was. Dark hair, wide shoulders and muscles to spare. He could snap her back like she was a toothpick and Cassie felt a second of fear but nothing showed on her face.

Walking around the side of his desk, he came close to where she stood. "So you don't like to be touched huh?" His steel colored eyes brined at her.

Cassie narrowed her eyes and took a step back. When he took a step forward, she could feel the power building up inside her. She matched his temper but she knew she couldn't match his brawn. Her mind zipped through defensive moves she'd used in the past. "No, I don't," she whispered. "I don't want to hurt you but I will if you force this."

Deke barked a laugh. "I don't think you could touch me but I could definitely hurt you."

"No man will ever hurt me again." She sneered. "I don't care how big, brawny or fucking stupid they happen to be."

Wiley gasped and paled. He watched with fear on his face waiting to see what Deke would do. No one, certainly not a woman had ever called this man stupid and lived.

But Deke surprised everyone by throwing his head back and laughing. When he stopped laughing, he looked her in the eye and said, "Lady, you have balls, I'll give you that. Just don't ever call me stupid again, or I *will* hurt you."

"You could try," she vowed under her breath. "Then don't act it and we'll get along fine," she said louder than before.

"I still need a name." Deke seemed calm and cool as he went back to his chair and sat down. Opening his desk drawer, he brought out a bottle of Black Velvet whiskey. Grabbing a couple of glasses, he poured out two shots and put one in front of her.

Cassie shook her head. "I don't drink, sorry."

Deke nodded. "What's your name?" he asked her for the third time.

"Cassie."

"Just Cassie?" he asked.

"Just Cassie. Kinda like just Cher or Madonna."

Deke glanced over at Wiley. "Why don't you find Peaches and bring her here."

Wiley nodded and left the room.

Deke motioned for Cassie to sit while she waited for her friend. "Is there something other than whiskey you would like to drink?"

"Black coffee works for me." Cassie sat down. "If you don't have that, water is good."

Deke looked over at Jack and nodded.

Jack got up and left the room.

"So, tell me about you and Peaches?" he asked as he poured another shot.

"We grew up together in the same hell hole until I got big enough to take care of the both of us. We've been together since we were five years old."

"How did you lose track of her then?" Deke looked curious.

"Some jackass snatched her off the street when she was coming home from work about three months ago." She glared at him. "I've been looking for her ever since."

Deke frowned. "She came here looking for work. I had nothing to do with how she got here. That ain't how we roll."

"I didn't say you were the jackass but somebody is and when I find them I intend to kill them," Cassie vowed.

~****~

Wiley entered the boarding house and went to Peaches' room.

When he knocked on the door, she called out with a sleepy, "Come in."

Wiley opened the door and found her in bed.

She raised her gaze to him and looked confused. "What are you doing here?"

"You got a visitor."

"A what?" Peaches asked as she got out of bed.

"Some dame is looking for you."

Peaches' nervous gaze focused on the bruise on his jaw. "Cassie is here, isn't she?"

"How did you know?"

Peaches smiled as she studied the bruises on his face. "She warned you not to touch her didn't she?" She laughed. "That girl."

Wiley grabbed her by the arm and squeezed. "That girl is in a whole mess of trouble. She's going head to head with Deke at the moment. If you mean as much to her as she thinks, you won't waste any more time. Let's get going."

Peaches looked upset as she rushed to get her clothes on and followed Wiley out the door.

When they entered the club, Hal nodded and Wiley grabbed her by the arm again, dragging her toward the back to Deke's office. Throwing open the door, he pushed Peaches inside.

Peaches stumbled and almost fell as she called out, "Cassie!"

Cassie turned and jumped to her feet. Rushing over to her friend, she hugged her. "I thought I'd never seen you again." Tears rolled down her face as she stared at the best friend she had in the world. The two of them had been through so much together. Taking a step back, she noted the faint bruising on Peaches' arms. Looking into her friend's eyes she asked, "Did he hurt you baby girl?"

Peaches glanced at Wiley and shook her head. "No, not really. These guys play rough but no, he didn't hurt me."

Cassie turned her head and glared at Deke. She sneered at him but didn't say anything. Then she turned her glare to Wiley. "If you touch her again, I will kill you."

Peaches gasped, turning to Wiley. "She didn't mean anything by that."

"The hell I didn't. You're not their plaything, to use and abuse. You are a dancer."

"Enough!" Deke shouted. "Who the fuck do you think you are, coming in here threatening my men? What gives you the right?"

"Who do I think I am?" Cassie shouted back as she stomped over to his desk. "I'm somebody who's sick to death of being threatened by big apes like you who thinks he can bully his way through life. I've had to scratch and claw my way every day and I don't take shit from nobody. Do you hear that? I won't take shit from you or your men." She raised her hand and slapped him.

The sound echoed in the office. Wiley gasped loudly as he took a step back.

Deke got to his feet again. Everyone could see the rage on his face as well as the red mark from her slap.

Peaches rushed forward and grabbed Cassie, pulling her back away from the desk. "She didn't mean it, Deke. Please don't hurt her," she begged.

Deke nodded to Wiley.

"Oh, no! Don't do it, Wiley!" Peaches yelled.

Pushing Peaches out of the way, he grabbed Cassie by the arms and crushed her to his chest.

Dropping forward, Cassie lifted her left foot and slammed it into his balls. When she felt his grip loosen, she jabbed her elbow into his gut and rammed her head back into his face.

Wiley dropped to the floor like a stone.

She stood there for a moment, her breathing deep, her chest heaving. The rage inside her was leaving. She glared at him. "I told you not to fucking touch me."

Deke watched stunned at the swiftness of her attack. Wiley was a man twice her size and a hell of a lot stronger than she was. But she had taken him on and defeated him as sure as she claimed she would.

Peaches reached out to her and grabbing her hands she whispered, "You'd better run before they kill you."

Cassie raised her hand to Peaches' cheek. "I don't run, remember?" She turned to Deke and squared her shoulders. "I didn't come here to make trouble, not for you, not for anyone. I told that bastard not to touch me but he didn't listen. All I wanted to do was find my friend and make sure she was all right. That's all I wanted."

"You realize the kind of trouble you're in now, don't you?" Deke asked her. "We can't let it be known that a woman took out our Sergeant at Arms. That just wouldn't look good."

Cassie sighed. "So what are my options here? If you promise not to hurt Peaches, I'll do what you say. I didn't start this thing but as I have no choice, I will honor whatever you decide my punishment should be for as long as I choose."

Deke thought for a moment then suggested, "You become property of the club."

Cassie frowned. "I will not become a whore."

"You will become whatever I tell you, you are," Deke reminded her.

Cassie stared at him for a moment before she declared, "You sir, are a fucking bastard. A rotten, fucking, cock sucking bastard."

Deke moved to stand in front of her. Raising his hand, he struck her across the face.

Cassie swayed but didn't move. Tears formed in her eyes but she wouldn't allow them to escape.

Deke glared at her for a minute then turned to Peaches. "Don't you have work to do?"

Peaches nodded and left the room in a hurry.

Deke motioned for his men to leave.

Jack and Jared helped Wiley to his feet and they lumbered out.

Deke then walked over to the door, closing it behind them.

Cassie heard the snap as he locked the door.

CHAPTER TWO

Deke leaned against the door and watched her. "What do you have against people touching you?" he finally asked.

"I don't like it."

"Why?"

Cassie shrugged. "I just don't, that's all. If you grew up like I did, you wouldn't like it either."

"Is this where I hear about your rotten childhood?" he asked with a roll of his eyes. "If so, please skip it. I've lived it, I know it by heart."

"Then you know how it is. There are some things you just don't put up with from other people."

"I should probably warn you, when we get to the clubhouse, you're going to have one very pissed off old lady after you when she sees what you've done to Wiley."

Cassie shrugged. "She'll get over it."

"Aren't you afraid of anything?"

Cassie raised her gaze to his. "If you let the fear take you, it wins and you lose. I try not to lose."

He studied her for a long moment. "Let's go get your stuff and get you settled," Deke finally said. "I've got business to deal with." He opened the door and ushered her through it. As they made their way through the dance hall, he told her to wait for him. He then walked over to his vice president Gator and said, "You need to talk to Peaches. Get any and all information from her that you can about Cassie. Don't hurt her, just ask her about her friend. Then bring her to the clubhouse later."

Gator nodded, then had to ask, "Did she really take Wiley down?"

Deke nodded. "Yep she did and faster than anyone I've ever seen. She's got this thing about being touched."

"Yeah, I heard from the other boys about that." Gator chuckled. "I'll see what I can find out from Peaches and let you know."

"You do that." Deke didn't look amused as he answered and walked away.

They walked out into the sunlight and Cassie brought her hand up to shade her eyes. Going to where she parked her jeep, she got in and waited while Deke went to his bike. When she heard his engine start up, she drove back to the motel.

When they arrived, she went to her room. She didn't seem to care if he followed her or not and he stayed right behind her as she opened her door. Without another word, she began packing up her things. When she was done, she carried her suitcase out to her jeep and waited. "I have to follow you to wherever it is you're taking me."

Deke stared at her for a moment and had to wonder if this was the smart thing to do. She owed him for her actions but he knew the club could be hard for an outsider. She wasn't used to being in a biker's club and it wasn't for everyone. There was also the backlash that would come from the old ladies about the beatings today. He shrugged. "Follow me and try not to get lost. I will chase your ass down."

Cassie glared at him. "You could try." Reaching over, she turned the key and started her engine.

~****~

When Deke pulled out of the parking lot, she followed him all the way to the outskirts of town and turning left, they traveled another couple of miles to a compound. There were several buildings behind a chain link and razor topped fence. Someone opened the front gate and she followed him inside. Turning the jeep off, she watched as a young man closed the gate behind them.

Then she felt Deke beside her. He grabbed her suitcase and led her inside the main building.

The inside was clean as she walked in. The floors were scrubbed and the walls were painted an off white color. To the left of the main doors was a huge kitchen and she could see several women standing there staring back at her.

To the right of the doors were tables, sofas and chairs. Several rather large men sat around and they too were staring at her. In front of the doors on the opposite wall was a long bar with row after row of bottles of alcohol and a couple of beer kegs.

Deke didn't say a word as he walked down the hall to the back of the main floor. He opened a door and she walked in.

It was a good sized room with a big bed and dresser. The walls had shelves filled with motorcycle parts and books. Off to the left was another door and when she opened it she could see a bathroom. There was a closet filled with men's clothes.

She turned to study Deke. "Whose room is this?"

"It's my room and you'll be sleeping here." He leaned against the door and waited for her to say something. He didn't wait very long.

"I will not be a whore. Not for you or anyone else."

"I remember something along those lines but I also remember telling you that you would become whatever I said you would be." Deke crossed his arms over his wide chest. "You told me you would honor the option the club made for you. Or is your word no good here?"

Cassie gritted her teeth. She'd always kept her promises. Her honor was all she had. "You're nothing more than a bully and a bastard."

Deke nodded. "Yes I am, but I'm also so much more than that." He held out his large hand. "I'll let you get settled in. I'll take the keys to your jeep now."

Cassie handed her keys over and moved over to the window. She didn't want him to see the fear in her eyes as she suddenly realized what her life had become. She heard the door close behind him and the snap of the lock as the tumblers turned. She took the blanket off the bed and went to the far corner of the room. Putting the blanket around her shoulders, she sat down on the floor and brought her knees to her chest.

Remembering the past, she felt the heat leave her body and soon, she was shivering from the coldness that came from her memories.

~****~

Deke made his way out to the main room and walked over to the bar. He nodded to the man behind it and accepted the glass of whiskey he was given. He was joined shortly by one of the women from the kitchen.

It was Wiley's old lady, Connie. "They brought Wiley home in the van. Someone beat the shit out of him and I want to know who did it."

Deke turned and stared at her. "What did Wiley tell you?"

"Wiley has busted balls, a broken nose and a bruise on his jaw." She seethed. "He told me some bitch tore him up but I don't believe that for a minute. No woman could do all that to someone his size."

Deke raised his glass to his lips. Taking a good swig, he let the liquor burn his throat and then he answered, "I didn't think so either but it happened. I was there when she did it."

Connie stared at him in shock. "Are you fucking kidding me?"

Deke shook his head. The clubhouse was filling up and everyone was taking note of their conversation. Deke looked around at everyone and said, "I strongly suggest you all keep your distance from the woman that just came in here. Cassie will protect herself and she won't care if you're female or male. She will take you down. She hates to be touched as Wiley, Jack and Jared found out earlier. I suggest for at least the time being, you all give her plenty of space."

"I'll give her the back of my hand." Connie growled.

"Connie, don't do it. I'd hate to see your pretty face all bruised up," Deke told her.

"She really took down three of us?" Killian asked in a hushed voice from behind the bar.

He nodded. "For now, don't push her and for god's sake, don't touch her. It sets her off."

The main doors opened and Gator came inside.

Deke then followed his VP down the hall and into his office. Closing the door behind them, Deke poured them both another drink. Looking at his second in charge he asked, "Well, what did you find out?"

Gator slammed the drink down and reached for the bottle. "Peaches told me very little. She said her name was Cassie and that they had gone through the foster system together. She said they both were ten years old when some bastard tried to rape her. Peaches that is, not Cassie. Cassie killed the man and they ran away together. They survived because of Cassie. They grew up on the streets and it wasn't easy. Cassie always promised to keep Peaches safe and until three months ago, she had."

Deke stared off into space for a moment then asked, "What happened three months ago?"

Gator snorted then poured himself and Deke another shot. "Some lowlife snatched Peaches off the street. He took her to a whorehouse and sold her to Big Jimmy. Then apparently, Big Jimmy used her until she got injured, then threw her out into the street. She heard about the dancehall and when she got better, she came looking for a job."

"What was wrong with her?" Deke asked.

"Some lowlife stabbed her when he was fucking her. She said she thought she was gonna die. Big Jimmy just dumped her along the highway. The next morning, she was found and taken to the hospital. She wouldn't tell them her name or what happened to her. When they patched her up, Peaches said she took off. She managed to find a place to hide until she was well enough to come here."

"What about Cassie? Did she say any more about her?"

Gator shook his head. "She said she wouldn't talk about her to anyone. She said if you want to know, you'll have to ask Cassie."

"Put a couple of guys on Peaches. I don't want anything to happen to her. If Big Jimmy knows where she's at, he might come looking for her."

Gator nodded. "What are you gonna do with the little Spitfire?"

Deke paused at the moniker, then he shrugged his wide shoulders. "I haven't made up my mind yet on that one. For now, I've warned everyone to steer clear of her. "

Gator grinned. "Yeah, I heard she can be a hellcat."

Deke laughed. "You have no idea." He shook his head. "If I hadn't seen it with my own eyes, I wouldn't have believed it. She took Wiley down the hard way...in about three seconds flat."

"Yeah, Peaches did mention Cassie doesn't like to be touched."

"She did warn him. Once at the motel and once in my office. I just never thought for a moment, she would do it with all of us standing there."

"I also hear she's got a mouth on her that won't quit." Gator kept grinning at his friend.

Deke stared at him for a moment then asked, "How many men do you know that would call me a jackass and live to tell about it?" He rubbed the side of his face remembering the slap she'd given him earlier.

Gator kept grinning as he poured them another drink, raised his glass and silently saluted the woman down the hall.

~*****~

Hours later, Deke unlocked the door to his room and went inside. He looked over at the bed but saw it was empty. Panicking for a moment, he snapped on the light. When he found her sitting in the corner, he shut the door and locked it again. Pushing the key into his pocket, he moved over to where she was sitting. "Are you okay?" he asked as he squatted down beside her. He didn't touch her but he knew she was aware of his presence.

Cassie raised her head and those intense green eyes of hers stared at him for a moment. Nodding her head, she lowered it back down on her knees.

Deke was strangely affected by the look in her eyes. So full of hurt and bewilderment, they made him feel like she'd given up hope. He moved over to the bed and began undressing. When he was naked, he walked over and turned off the light. He slept in the raw, always had. Just as long as his gun was within reach, then he would be able to chill. Settling in the big king size bed, he told her, "You can sleep here with me. I won't bother you tonight."

She didn't respond and Deke slowly settled in for some sleep. He thought he heard her crying but the sounds were too soft to hear clearly. He wouldn't bother her. For some reason he couldn't define, he wanted to give her a feeling she could trust him. He closed his eyes and went to sleep.

~* * * *~

It was like that for the next few days. Every morning, Deke got up and went to work, while Cassie stayed at the clubhouse. Every night, she slept in the corner while he slept in the bed. No one bothered her and she didn't bother them. She spent her day watching everything that went on around her. Her nights were spent sleeping in his room but she was still all alone.

The fourth night, found Cassie sitting in the same corner of the room. She sat there for a while, softly weeping. When she heard him begin to snore, she got up and went over to the bed. Staring down at him, she marveled at the sight of him. He was bigger than most men she knew and stronger. His chest and arms were rock solid. In the moonlight, she could see many patches of black on his skin. She couldn't make out what the tattoos were but she could see he had them.

She was tired of being alone and studied him as he slept. His face looked softer than it did when he was awake and she could make out the shape of his eyes and nose. His lips looked softer too, and she wondered how they would feel on her skin if he kissed her.

Cassie thought about that. She didn't know much about love, never having experienced it before. After what happened to Peaches when they were ten, she made sure no one ever touched her that way. She had always protected herself and Peaches up until three months ago. Then when she learned a few weeks ago what happened to her friend she had paid Big Jimmy a visit.

When he saw her, he told her she could take Peaches' place in his stable and when she said no, he hadn't believed her. He too, learned the hard way she didn't like to be touched and it was a lesson she knew he would never forget.

She sat down on the bed.

Deke opened his eyes and saw her sitting there. Then turned his back to her.

Cassie felt him turn away but she was too tired to think anymore. Life had beaten her down and she needed some rest. Wrapping the blanket around her shoulders, she laid on top of the blankets next to him on the large bed and closed her eyes. Sleep took her and a few tears rolled down her cheeks.

~*****~

Deke waited for a while then turned very carefully. He saw the tears on her cheeks and closing his eyes, he went back to sleep. He hoped the morning would be better. He didn't believe for a moment that tears were Cassie's way to deal with anything life had to offer.

A few hours later, just as the dawn was breaking Deke felt something soft and gentle touch his skin. At first, he wasn't sure what it was. Then he felt it again. He opened his eyes slightly and found himself staring into bright green eyes. It was her fingers touching his face. He watched as she ran her hands along his jaw.

She hesitated to touch him any further and then she touched his lips.

Her soft hands barely touched him but he felt the burn of her tiny hands as she outlined his lips. "I thought you didn't like to be touched?" he whispered.

"You aren't touching me, I'm touching you." Staring at him she asked, "Can I kiss you?"

Deke felt surprised but he nodded. Ever so softly, she leaned toward him. He waited as she stared at his lips then she came even closer. Her lips touched his hesitantly. It raised his curiosity. It was as if she'd never kissed anyone before. He waited while she explored his lips with hers. When she got bolder, he opened his mouth and let her tongue thrust inside.

She moaned at her own actions.

The kiss was getting hotter but Deke didn't move to touch her. He let her kiss him. He groaned as her hands cupped his face. Her lips began kissing his chin, working their way to his neck and chest.

When she suddenly stopped and pushed herself off him, she stared at him. "Was that okay?"

Deke swallowed and stared back at her. "Was what okay?"

"The kiss. I've never done that before, so I didn't know what to do."

Deke frowned. "What do you mean never before?"

"I've never kissed anyone before. I didn't know how to do it." She glanced at him then looked away again. "Did I do it right?"

Deke raised his hand slowly. Barely touching her chin, he brought her face toward his. He studied her for a moment then said, "You did just fine." She blushed and he had to ask, "How old are you anyway?"

Cassie blushed redder. "I'm twenty two." She stared out the window for a moment, then turned back to look at him. "Can we kiss again?"

Deke hid the smile that wanted to break over his lips and nodded. "I think I'd like that."

Cassie leaned toward him. Her tongue licked her dry lips and Deke groaned. Without thinking about it, he raised up and turned her over on her back. Grabbing her face, he lowered his lips to hers and when she opened her mouth to gasp, his tongue entered. They kissed long and deep.

His body was hot against hers, separated only by the blanket between them. She groaned as his hands lowered to her shoulders. Pushing the blanket from her, Deke's eyes widened as he noted her bare skin beneath it. He knew she had been fully clothed when they had fallen asleep but now she was bare to him.

His hands shook as he removed the blanket and took in the sight of her. He knew he needed to be very careful and not mess this up. He wasn't used to having to be cautious and gentle, not in his life. Her skin was creamy white and soft. He gently traced her shoulder bones and watched her breathe. Her breasts were full and tight. Her chest moved quickly as his hands lowered to her belly. His fingers skimmed her flat stomach and he lowered them further still until he touched her mound.

His fingers tangled gently in the red curls that hid her womanhood from the world. Ever so gently, he leaned over and licked her breast. Her nipple hardened in response and she moaned at the unfamiliar feelings coursing through her body. His fingers then brushed against her clit and she jumped. "Shhh, don't panic, just let the feelings through," he whispered in her ear.

Cassie nodded and his fingers brushed her clit again. She moaned and opened her legs wider. "Please...?" she whispered.

Deke groaned and leaned closer to her breast. His lips sucked her nipple in deep. She cried out as his fingers ran down her slit. He opened her nether lips and ran his finger along it. He could feel the wetness and he groaned again. Dammit, this woman was a treasure and one he needed to go very slowly with—if he could hold his lust back.

Slipping a finger inside her, he began fingering her. Deeper and deeper with each thrust, he could feel her body tighten against him.

When he slipped another finger inside her, she moaned and began moving her hips to his rhythm.

He suckled her breast then changed to the other side. His cock was harder than it had ever been before and was screaming for release. His fingers went deeper and he could feel a small patch of skin barring the way. Deke knew he shouldn't be surprised but his heart soared at its presence. "I need to fuck you," he whispered. "I need you so much it hurts." He gazed intently at her. "Are you ready for that?"

Cassie nodded. "Show me what passion is like."

He moved to lay between her legs. He was so ready and he prayed she was too. He put his cock at her opening and pushed inside slowly. Hissing, he told her, "You're so tight." When he got to the point he could go no further without causing her pain, he leaned over and sucked her nipple into his mouth again. Biting down he heard her hiss of pain and he moved inside her. Pushing past the pain and her sign of innocence, he felt her buck against him.

Easing himself the rest of the way in, he slowly brought himself out, then he pushed deeper and set the rhythm he wanted. His lips nibbled on her neck and he could feel her body responding to his thrusts. Soon, she cried out and arching her back, he felt her gripping his cock as her orgasm hit her. His control snapped and with a few more strokes, deeper and harder than before, Deke joined her. He almost growled as he felt his body let go.

Sweat beaded his forehead and a drop splashed down onto her chest. He rested a moment on his elbows before moving to her side. "Are you all right?" he asked gently.

Turning her head, she smiled. "I never knew sex would feel that good."

"That was pretty amazing," he agreed.

"Is it always that good?"

"I guess that depends on who you're with when it happens. It's different with each partner you have."

"I don't want to be with anyone else." She frowned. "I just want to be with you."

Deke shrugged. "It doesn't always work that way, sweet thing."

Cassie closed her eyes. Rolling away from him, she gathered up her blanket and ran into the bathroom.

Deke flopped back down on the bed. He'd been amazed at what transpired this morning. He couldn't believe she'd never known the touch of a man before today. He'd thought that would have been the reason she didn't like to be touched, that some man had brutalized her, but that hadn't been the case. He was even more mystified now than before.

What they had done here had been nothing short of spectacular. Never before had he had such a response as the one she gave him. Her touch had been awesome and her body had been more than he ever hoped to be on the receiving end of. The scent of her arousal had driven him crazy. He brought the fingers to his mouth that had been buried deep within her. Touching his lips to them, he could still taste her. Like her juices were made for him, a flavor he now craved.

Deke groaned and pushed himself out of bed. If he thought about her much longer, he would need her again for round two. He needed to clear his head. Pulling his pants on, he grabbed a shirt and left the room. Making his way down the hall, he noticed Honey and Reva were in the kitchen getting coffee going.

Honey, River's old lady smiled when she saw him. "Morning, Deke."

"Morning."

Reva, Gator's wife, handed him a cup of the hot brew.

Deke grinned and said, "Thank you, darlin."

Reva blushed slightly and went back to work gathering items for the breakfast meal they served to those who wanted it.

Deke turned and went to join Gator at one of the tables. They were quiet for a while, each lost in his own thoughts.

Finally, Gator cleared his throat and glanced over at Deke.

Deke noted his vice president staring at him. "What's on your mind, Gator?"

"Heard a rumor a few nights back and I can't make up my mind as to whether or not to believe it."

Deke glanced over at Gator. "What kind of rumor?"

Gator rubbed his earlobe between his fingers as he looked troubled. "Somebody said that Big Jimmy was in the hospital. Heard someone had almost cut his manhood off a few weeks ago. Heard too, he was in real bad shape, lost a lot of blood."

Deke thought about what Gator told him then glanced down the hall toward his bedroom. He couldn't help but wonder about this news. He lifted his cup to his mouth and sipped the coffee. "Interesting news, isn't it?"

"Yup, it sure is. Kinda makes a person wonder though."

"Wonder about what?"

"How somebody could do that," Gator explained. "That would be a terrible thing to happen to a man."

"It would indeed," Deke agreed. "But it also has to make you wonder what Big Jimmy did to bring out that kind of rage in someone. Don't you think?"

Gator nodded. "It is a mystery isn't it?"

Deke drank his coffee and enjoyed the silence around him for a few minutes anyway. Then he saw his door open and Cassie walked out. He glanced over at Reva and lifted his cup.

Reva grabbed the coffee pot, an extra cup and brought it to the table. She poured the coffee and went back to the kitchen, never bothering to look at the person sitting beside Deke.

Cassie raised the cup to her lips and moaned as the hot brew slid down her throat. "Man, that is great coffee," she said to no one in particular.

"Yup, my woman can make a great cup of coffee in the mornings," Gator commented.

Cassie looked at the him sitting there and smiled slightly. Holding out her hand, she said, "I'm Cassie."

Gator stared at her for a moment then reached out to take her hand. "I'm Gator."

A short time later, people began gathering inside the clubhouse. One or two at a time until soon, all the tables were filled. Wiley limped in last. His arm was around a slender woman and when she noticed Cassie, she glared at her. Her fingers rolled into a fist and she growled. Wiley whispered something to her and glanced over at Cassie. Then he kissed the woman's head and went over to a table in the corner of the room.

Cassie stared at him for a moment then turned her gaze to the kitchen area where she found Wiley's woman was glaring at her. Cassie turned to Deke.

He shrugged. "I did warn everyone to leave you alone but Connie might not listen."

Cassie nodded. Getting to her feet, she made her way over to where Wiley was sitting. Wiley stared at her the whole way. When she reached him she said, "I'm sorry I hurt you the other day."

Before Wiley had a chance to say anything, Cassie turned and found Wiley's woman standing there with a knife in her hand.

"Get away from my man." Connie snarled. "Get away from him and stay away from him!"

"Connie, back the fuck off," Wiley told her. "She isn't here to do anything to me."

"I came to apologize to him," Cassie told them.

"I ought to gut you like a fish." Connie hissed. "I ought to cut you real bad and watch you bleed all over the floor."

~****~

Cassie cocked her head and felt herself shutting down. Going into survival mode, she watched the woman holding the knife carefully.

Everyone around them went silent as they watched the drama unfold.

"Deke," she called out. "I don't want to spill any blood here today. I just want you to know that."

"I know that darlin," Deke called back. "I did warn her not to mess with you."

Wiley got to his feet and walked around Cassie. He stepped between Cassie and his woman. He tried to take the knife out of her hands.

Connie pushed him away. "This bitch needs a lesson."

Wiley grabbed Connie and pulled her back. "Don't do this woman. Let it go."

Connie struggled to get away from him. When she succeeded, she turned to Cassie and began moving forward. No one tried to stop her now. Connie brought the knife out in front of her and crouched slightly.

Cassie didn't move a muscle. "Please don't do this. I don't want to hurt you."

Connie scoffed. "But I want to hurt you. I want to fucking kill you!"

Cassie raised her eyes to Wiley.

Seeing her distracted, Connie struck. She brought the knife into position and jabbed at Cassie. Cassie moved to avoid the blade. Connie followed, swinging the blade a third time. Cassie reached out and knocked it away from Connie.

Cassie stepped to one side and Connie rushed past her. She bent over and grabbed the knife again, then went after Cassie. Cassie blocked the knife a few more times and that enraged Connie, so she swung the blade again and this time, she nicked Cassie's arm.

Everyone watched as the expression changed on Cassie's face. Her eyes narrowed and her skin paled as she breathed a little deeper.

Deke called out softly, "Cassie, don't kill her."

Cassie nodded distractedly and went on the attack. She jabbed her fist in the other woman's face and Connie swung away with the force of the hit. Then Cassie raised her leg to kick at her, again and again, striking the woman in several key places: her gut, her chest and her ass. Her intent hadn't been to kill but to injure her opponent. The third time she struck Connie with a direct smack to the temple, the other woman fell to the floor, dazed.

Cassie stood over her, her hands clenched into fists, her breathing deep as rage took her. Finally, Cassie pushed it away. She raised her gaze to stare at Wiley.

He looked pale. His eyes were on his woman and when he swung his gaze up to Cassie, he mouthed a silent, *"Thank you."*

Connie laid on the floor in pain. She'd truly never seen Cassie coming.

When Cassie walked away, Wiley bent down and helped her up off the floor. Wrapping his arms around her, he helped her to the table and sat down.

Honey ran out of the kitchen with a basin of water and a washcloth. The women worked to clean her up.

Cassie glanced over at Deke and Gator to say, "I didn't mean to make her mad. I wanted to apologize to Wiley for my actions. I hope I didn't hurt her too badly."

Deke raised an eyebrow and shook his head. "I think you made your point loud and clear. You gave her ample warning."

Cassie shook her head. "Doesn't make what I did right. I didn't have to hit her so many times." She lowered her head and her voice dropped to a whisper. "But when the rage takes me, I can't stop." She got to her feet and ran toward the bedroom. The door slammed behind her and the entire room was silent.

Gator looked over at Deke. "Wow. I've never seen those kinds of moves before. I thought sure as shit, Connie was gonna kill her."

"Same thing happened the other day when Wiley grabbed her. She just went ballistic on him." Deke shook his head.

"Yeah, that's what I heard, so I didn't want to touch her myself." Gator laughed. "I guess it's fine if she touched me first by shaking my hand, huh? What a spitfire!"

"Spitfire?" Deke laughed.

Reva brought out the coffee pot again, and filled their cups. "Do you think she'll want some more?" she asked softly.

"Can I take it to her?" a voice came from behind Deke.

They turned their heads and saw Peaches standing there.

She nodded at two men standing just inside the door. "I asked them to bring me here, so I could talk to Cassie."

"Did you see what she did?" Deke asked as he motioned for her to sit.

Peaches nodded as she sat at the table. "She's got better control of her rages than she did a few years ago."

"What does that mean?" Deke frowned.

"It means she didn't kill anyone or even half kill them," Peaches said quietly.

"Explain that to me." Deke glared at her.

"Cassie's life was a living hell when I first met her. We were both five years old and every day she got beat up by our foster mother. When the pain from her slapping didn't mean anything anymore, she graduated to a belt. Then a whip. It was rough on all of us but she enjoyed beating Cassie the most. Cassie stuck up for the other kids you see. She would always take their punishment and that drove Mrs. Pierce crazy mad."

"Go on," Deke ordered her to continue.

Peaches shook her head. "Cassie took it for five very long years and she would have taken it longer if Robbie Pierce hadn't tried to rape me. She didn't let him do that."

"What happened?" Gator asked.

"She cut him real bad," Peaches whispered. "There was so much blood. When she finished, she grabbed my hand and we ran away. She vowed she would always protect me and she did. No one messed with Cassie. She kept us both safe for a long time."

Reva set a fresh cup of coffee down and patted her on the arm. She tilted her head. "You tell her breakfast will be ready soon."

Peaches got up and taking the coffee, she went to the back room.

Gator watched her go, then turned to Deke. "Kinda makes sense now doesn't it? Her not wanting to be touched."

"Yeah, it does. It also makes me wonder why social services didn't notice the kids were getting beaten." The whole thing left a bad taste in his mouth.

CHAPTER THREE

Peaches knocked on the door and opened it carefully. She saw her friend sitting in the corner wrapped up in a blanket and it reminded her so much of the past, she almost cried. "Oh Cassie, what have they done to you?"

"Peaches, I'm in so much trouble!" Cassie wailed.

Peaches ran over to where she sat and wrapped her arms around her. "No, you're not. They don't know. I swear I would never say anything to put you in harm's way."

"But you had to tell them something."

"I told them you were beaten everyday by that bitch Mrs. Pierce and I told them about the day we ran away but that's all, I swear," Peaches cried.

Cassie nodded. "We can't tell them anything more. We have to protect our secret."

Peaches nodded. "I will. I won't tell them, I promise."

Cassie stayed in Peaches' arms for the longest time. Then she peeked up at her friend and smiled. "I kissed him this morning," she whispered.

Peaches swallowed hard. "Who did you kiss?"

"Deke."

"Oh, honey," Peaches said softly. "Is that really wise?"

"I don't know if it was wise but oh, it felt so wonderful."

"Did you fuck him?" Peaches asked with a fearful look on her face.

"Yup and it felt great," Cassie admitted.

For a long time neither of them spoke then Cassie said, "I didn't mind his touch. In fact. it didn't feel so bad."

"Oh, baby." Peaches wrapped her arms tighter around her. "Some touches are okay and others are wonderful. Not everyone's touches hurt."

"I know that now. His touch didn't hurt me."

"I'm glad." Peaches brushed Cassie's hair away from her face. "Come on girl, Reva said breakfast would be ready soon."

Cassie got to her feet and laid the blanket back on the bed. She followed Peaches to the door and back into the main room. Deke's table was full, so they went over to another table and sat down.

Reva carried them each a plate of food and after setting it on the table, she glanced at Cassie. "I hope you'll give us a chance to be friends. Not all of us are as crazy as Connie."

Cassie nodded. "I understand why she did what she did. I hope she can understand something as well. I did tell him not to touch me. In fact, I told him twice. He didn't listen either time."

Peaches smiled at her.

Reva laughed. "Bet he'll listen now."

"I hope someday, he can forgive me," Cassie said.

"Forgive you?" Reva asked. "What does he need to forgive?"

"My mama told me when I was really young, it was wrong to hurt people. I really try not to, that's why I tell them not to touch me."

"When did you lose your mama?" Reva asked.

"I was three I think when she died."

"Oh honey, I'm sorry." Reva reached her hand out but didn't make contact.

Cassie took her hand and squeezed it. "It's okay, her hell ended and mine began," she whispered. Then she picked up her fork and began eating.

~****~

Reva got up and walked back to the kitchen with tears in her eyes.

A few minutes later, Gator walked in and wrapped his arms around her.

"That poor child," Reva whispered sadly.

"Can you try and make friends with her, baby? Deke wants to know more about her. He thinks she's hiding from someone and he wants to know who it is. If it's gonna bring the badges down on us, we need to know."

"Yeah baby, I can ask her." Reva rested her cheek on the big man's shoulders for a moment, then she pushed him away. "You'd better finish your meal and go do whatever it is you guys do. I have work to do."

Gator's lips crashed down on hers and they took a moment out for their own pleasure. Finally, he broke the kiss. "Woman, you taste so fine."

"Remember that tonight. I'll be the one laying in your bed." Reva chuckled.

"You'll be the only one I'll be fucking for the rest of my life."

"You got that right, mister." Reva swatted him on the ass as he walked away.

Cassie brought their plates back to the kitchen and asked if she could help clean up.

Reva nodded and watched as she began washing the mountain of dishes sitting by the sink. "Where did your friend go?"

"Peaches had to go to work. She's a dancer in the club."

"Did you have a job before you came here?" Reva asked.

"Yup I did. I used to work in a law office."

"A law office?" Reva was startled. "Whatever did you do there?"

"I was working on becoming a paralegal. Peaches and I got our GED's when we were sixteen. I took some classes at night, when we had the money and worked during the day. Peaches and I were going to make a good life for ourselves. I had to quit my job when Peaches was taken. I had to find her and make sure she was okay."

"Sounds like you were busy."

"Busy isn't always a bad thing. After my classes were done, I made time to paint a little."

"Paint?" Reva asked, "What did you paint?"

"Would you like to see?" Cassie turned to Reva. "If you don't tell anyone I'll show you my drawings."

Reva nodded and they went down the hall to the bedroom she shared with Deke.

Cassie got her suitcase from the closet and opened it. From under her clothes, she pulled out a book. She studied Reva for a long moment. "Please don't tell anyone what you see in this book. It's my secret."

Reva took the book from her and promised, "I won't tell anyone." She sat down on the bed and opened the book. She gasped at page after page of excellent drawings. They were so realistic she couldn't grasp it really. Each was a face of a homeless person, or the face of a tiny baby resting. The best drawings though, were in the back of the book. Cassie liked to draw big cats. Lions and tigers mostly but each drawing seemed so real. "These are really good."

Cassie smiled. "Thanks."

"Why do you hide them?"

She shrugged. "I don't know. Most people wouldn't understand my passion for drawing. I can get lost for hours once I start drawing. I tend to get carried away when the right mood hits me." She sighed. "They look at me and see a misfit, a nobody."

"Oh baby girl, you are somebody very special." Reva closed the book.

"If I'm so special, how come nobody out there but Peaches loves me?" Cassie whispered. "Why did my mom have to die and why did my dad throw me away?" Tears rolled down her cheeks.

Reva held out her arms and waited for Cassie. When she joined her, Reva held the girl close and just let her cry. "Honey, I don't know what to tell you. Some people are just plain stupid and some others just give up trying after so long. I'm sure your mom didn't want to leave you, she just couldn't stay with you anymore."

Cassie left the haven of Reva's arms. "What is it with you people? I didn't even cry this much when I was a kid." She brushed her tears away.

Reva smiled and shook her head. "Sometimes, we all need to cry. There is nothing wrong with that."

"But tears don't do anyone any good," she insisted as she swiped the tears from her cheeks.

"Sometimes, we need the tears to cleanse our souls. Tears can wash away the pain we feel at times."

Cassie shrugged and looked down at the wound on her arm that Connie left her with. She had stopped the bleeding before but now fresh blood stained her arm. "Oh, damn." She went to the bathroom and washed the blood from her skin. Going to her suitcase, she brought out a small first aid kit. Rummaging through it, she found a large band aid.

"Maybe you should lay down for a while?" Reva suggested. "You look a little tired."

"Yeah, I guess I am a little tired." Cassie laid down and throwing the blanket over her shoulders, she closed her eyes.

Reva slipped out of the bedroom and went back to the kitchen to finish up after the morning meal.

~* * * *~

Deke glared at the girl across from him. He was back at the club and Peaches wasn't cooperating with him this morning. "Why won't you tell me what I want to know?" he asked her for the third time.

Peaches had tears in her eyes. "I can't. If you want to know, you have to ask Cassie."

"Why?" he demanded. "She isn't going anywhere and I need to know if someone is coming after her. I can't protect her and the club if I don't know what I'm dealing with. She can't leave the compound, so tell me what I need to know."

Peaches chuckled despite the fear she felt. "I will tell you one thing, if Cassie wants to leave she will. Not even you can hold her."

Deke stared hard at her. "That would be impossible. No one has ever escaped the compound before."

"If you upset her, she will leave. I've seen her do it before. You won't even know she's gone until it's too late and then you won't find her, if she doesn't want you to."

"Tell me what I want to know." He growled.

"I can't!" Peaches wailed. "It's not my secret to share." She got to her feet and ran out of the room.

Deke groaned with frustration. He didn't know any more about the woman than he did when she came here. There had to be a way to find out something about her. No one was invisible.

He picked up the phone and called in a marker. When the contact answered, he told him what he wanted and the man on the other end hung up. Deke steepled his fingers and was deep in thought when Gator entered a few minutes later. "What's up?' he asked.

"That rumor we talked about this morning?" Gator reminded him.

"What about it?"

"It's now a fact. Big Jimmy died a couple of hours ago. The cops have no clue who cut him and neither does his crew. But his crew is very interested in who cut him up so badly."

"Are you sure?"

"Yep, his crew is sending feelers out all over town for information leading to the person or persons unknown who did the deed. Nobody knows what happened that night and Big Jimmy never regained consciousness to tell anybody anything."

"But we don't even know for sure she did it, do we?"

Gator shook his head. "We don't know that she didn't do it either. Did Peaches tell you anymore?"

"She won't give up any more info. She says it's not her secret to share and that if I want more about Cassie, I have to ask Cassie."

"Want I should lean on her a bit?"

Deke shook his head. "She also tells me Cassie can leave the compound anytime she wants and for some reason, I believe she can and will if Peaches gets hurt."

"And you don't want to lose her just yet, is that it?" Gator gave him an amused look.

Deke grinned. "That's about it."

"Good luck with that my brother." Gator chuckled. "Some women are a real bitch."

"That thought did cross my mind a time or two." Deke poured them a drink. "There's just something about this one. I can't put my finger on it but I know it's there."

"What else are you going to do?"

"I put a call into Rusty. He said it shouldn't be too hard to find her, if she was in the system. He said he would call back the day after tomorrow with any new info."

"Why do I have a feeling you ain't gonna like what you find out?" Gator reasoned.

"We'll soon know." Deke shrugged. "At least we'll know what we're dealing with."

~*****~

Cassie woke from her nap refreshed. She got up and went out into the main room. No one was there to bother her, so she decided to explore. In one of the backrooms, she found several cans of paint. Mostly black but there was a can or two of red and orange and green paint as well.

The rest of the rooms in the back were storage rooms and of no interest, so she passed them by. She opened another door and peered down into a black basement. She quickly shut the door. She had no interest at all in going down there. Basements terrified her.

She heard someone behind her and when she turned, she saw Connie standing there. "What's the matter bitch, scared of the dark?" She sneered.

Cassie didn't speak to her but instead walked away without saying a word. She didn't want to start anything.

Connie glared at her as she walked away.

When Cassie arrived in the main room, she paused and stared at the blank wall beside the bar. She had gotten an idea when she'd seen the paint. She could put her talents to good use and pray no one minded too much. It would certainly help the décor out a little. The clubhouse was a bit on the drab side.

Going into the bedroom she shared with Deke, she grabbed her notebook and opening it to a new page, she began drawing one of the two designs she wanted to paint on the walls. She'd have to wait until everyone else was asleep, so she needed to make sure the drawings were simple enough to get done in a few hours.

By the time she was done, she heard the roar of motorcycles in the courtyard. She was very happy with her designs. Putting her book back in her suitcase, Cassie went back out to the main room and joined the other women in the kitchen.

They were all busy getting things started for the evening meal.

"What can I do to help?" Cassie asked.

Reva grinned. "How good are you at cooking for a lot of hungry men?"

"I can do that." Cassie grinned back. "What's on the menu?"

"Surprise us." Reva nodded. "You're in charge of dinner tonight."

Cassie took her up on her challenge. "Is there anything the guys won't eat?"

Reva huffed. "As long as it's hot and filling, they won't care."

"Okay then everybody out. I need the kitchen." Cassie shooed them all out.

"Don't you need help?" Honey asked. "It usually takes all of us to feed this crew."

"Nope. I can handle it," Cassie assured them. "I was exploring today and found everything I need."

Reva took off her apron and nodded toward the door. "Ok, you heard her, she can do this on her own. Let's go have a drink with our men."

Cassie locked the door behind them and set to work. When she had explored the pantry, she found the ingredients for a recipe she hadn't made in years. One of her jobs as a kid was working in a restaurant and she found she was good at cooking.

Soon, the rich aroma of tomato sauce filled the kitchen. As the doors and windows were closed, she hoped no one else could smell the sauce. Soon, she was filling the six oversized pans with layers of noodles, sauce and cheese. The lasagna she was making was her own special creation. That along with the garlic bread and salad would be enough to fill everyone's stomach.

At five thirty on the dot, she raised the opening to the main room and everyone gathered around. She waited as everyone filled their plates and moved away to eat. Filling her own plate, she sat in the kitchen eating all alone.

Reva joined her a while later with a big smile on her face. "Supper was really great. Everybody, and I do mean *everybody* loved it. Gator, that old pig had four helpings." She groaned. "I ate too much myself. You made my Italian grandmother cry tonight."

Cassie smiled. "I made my Irish grandmother cry too."

Reva nodded. "You did the cooking, the rest of us will do the dishes."

Cassie walked over and joined the rest of the group. Deke motioned for her to join him and she went over to his table.

"I understand you cooked supper by yourself tonight. Why?" He stared at her.

"Old family recipe. I couldn't share the ingredients upon penalty of death."

Deke glared at her. "Not funny."

"Not intended to be." She shrugged. "Just the truth."

"Whatever it was, I've never tasted anything finer," Gator complimented her.

"Thank you. Now, if you'll excuse me I have something to do." She got up and began walking away when Deke grabbed her arm. Cassie tensed and tried not to show her fear as sweat began forming on her forehead.

Deke seemed to realize his mistake and carefully released her. "Please sit down for a moment with us. We have something to talk about."

Cassie sat down carefully. She had to stop and breathe for a minute. When she could focus again, she turned her gaze to Deke and regarded him with caution. "What can I do for you?"

~****~

Deke flushed. He shouldn't have to explain anything to anyone but she made him feel about three feet tall and that bothered him. For his whole life, his size and his attitude prevented any such nonsense of his ego ever being bruised. This little spitfire knew just what buttons to push. He paused...Spitfire? Damn that Gator and his nicknames. He motioned the bartender to bring a bottle and when he did, he poured himself a stiff drink.

Gator joined him and he poured a glass for Cassie.

Cassie ignored the drink in front of her.

After he finished his second glass, Deke scowled at her untouched drink. "What's the matter little Miss Prissy pants, are you too good to share a drink with us?" His words were slurry and his eyes were glazing over. He was well on his way to being drunk.

"I don't drink. I believe I told you that the other day," Cassie reminded him quietly.

Deke closed his eyes as her words slammed home. He felt almost ashamed of himself but if he let this drop, he would have discontent among his men. For some reason, he couldn't let this go. He had to show her who was boss. It was saving face. He was the prez here and he wouldn't put up with bullshit "Drink it." He growled.

"Deke...maybe she shouldn't." Gator tried to reason with him.

Deke just glared at him. "I said drink it," he insisted.

Cassie raised her head. "No."

"I can make you do it if I have to," he warned her.

Cassie shook her head. "God doesn't argue with sinners, drunks or fools."

Deke's jaw dropped and he stared at her. "Did you just call me a fool?"

"No I didn't. I said God doesn't argue with sinners, drunks or fools," Cassie insisted.

"Get the fuck away from me before I beat you." Deke growled, glaring at her.

"Gladly." She turned to leave.

He thought she called him an asshole but he didn't know for sure. Deke watched her go and when he turned around he saw Gator's chest shaking with mirth. "Don't you dare laugh at me, you big bastard."

Gator tried to contain his laughter. "I wouldn't dream of it."

"She needs to learn her place," Deke argued. "That's what I'll do, teach her what her place is."

"Ahh, Deke, Maybe you better finish your drink first," Gator suggested.

Deke nodded. "Maybe...That's a good idea." He reached for the bottle and poured them both another drink.

Gator sat beside him and they both got totally shitfaced.

An hour or so later, the clubhouse was quiet. Everyone else had gone to bed. Deke was snoring as he slept with his head on his folded arms on the table.

Reva was helping Gator stand up. "You damn old fool," she whispered. "Come on big boy, let's get you to bed."

"Sorry baby, I had to save his life tonight. That little girl would have killed him. She was plenty pissed at him the way it was."

"I know I saw her too." Reva accepted his reasoning. "You did good, baby. Maybe they needed this."

"I think the big guy is falling for her, honey." Gator slurred. "I don't know if that's good or bad but it could be a good thing, don't you think?"

Reva patted his stomach. "Yeah baby, that could be a good thing." She closed the door behind them and stumbled their way to the cottage next door.

~****~

Cassie waited until all was quiet. Deke hadn't come to bed yet, so she opened the door and walked to the main room. There he was, sleeping on the table. She went over to where he was sitting and poked him. When he didn't move, she let him alone.

Moving quietly, she gathered what she needed and she began to paint. Everything else disappeared as the lines of her patterns began forming. She lost track of everything around her as she got into her work. She finished the first piece and began the second almost without thinking about it.

As the night crawled closer to the early morning, her muscles began to ache. Her shoulders and arms began to tire and after she painted the last little bit, she dropped her paintbrush into the empty can and stood back to view her work.

"Wow girl, you got some talent there."

The words were spoken softly but they made Cassie jump and spin around.

Reva stood there gazing at what she'd done in awe. "You did all this in a few hours?" she exclaimed.

Cassie nodded as she picked up her empty can and went into the kitchen. Running water, she rinsed out the brush and threw away the can. Coming back into the main room, she asked, "Do you think anyone will care that I painted their walls?"

Reva turned her head and grinned. "I think they will love it. You did a great job. I can't wait until Gator sees this. He's gonna love it."

Cassie yawned. "I think I can sleep now. See you later."

"Yeah, you need to get some rest." She patted Cassie on the shoulder.

Cassie was too tired to care as she made her way down the hall. A few minutes later, she laid down on the bed fully dressed, closed her eyes and fell asleep.

~* * * *~

Deke groaned as he heard dishes slamming in the kitchen. His dreams had been weird. He dreamt of being chased by a huge snarling tiger all night. That and sounds of someone pacing behind him. It was certainly a dream he'd never had before. His bleary eyes focused on the empty bottle of Black Velvet sitting on the table and he vowed never to get that drunk again.

Picking up his head, he winced when someone set down a cup of coffee beside his head. The aroma almost made him want to puke. He had to take several deep breaths before the nausea disappeared. He groaned and sat up. Grabbing the coffee, it took both hands to bring it to his lips this morning. He groaned again, when the first sip slid down his throat.

"How are you feeling?" Reva asked as she sat down with her own cup of coffee.

"Am I still alive?" Deke jokingly asked her. "I had the weirdest dream last night. Something about being chased through the jungle by a huge assed tiger. I could hear the beast snarling at me all night long.

Reva snorted. "Look behind you, boss."

Deke glared at her but turned his head and simply stared. He slowly got to his feet, never taking his eyes off the beast. The tiger in his dreams had come to life and it was standing about three feet away. He could see its snarl, he could almost hear its mighty roar. "What the fucking hell is that?" he cried out as he backed away from it.

Reva laughed. "It isn't going to hurt you, you know. She worked on it all night. Isn't it great?"

Deke's swiftly beating heart slowed down as he stared at the painting on the wall. The tiger seemed so real it was uncanny. He seemed to be leaping off of the wall straight at him. Then he turned his head and saw the other painting. There on the wall bigger than life was the Satan's Spawn patch. The colors were bold and bright and it too seemed three dimensional. "Wow, are you telling me that Cassie painted this?"

"Yep, she's got some kinda talent." Reva sipped her coffee.

The main door opened and Gator stumbled inside. His head was drooping and he could barely put one foot in front of the other. When he sat down, he glanced at his wife and begged her, "Please woman, get me coffee. I need it strong and black this morning."

Reva got up and fetched a pot. When she sat down, she poured him a cup and set it close to his head. When he raised his head, something caught his eye and he sat up with a start. "What the fuck?" he called out as he stared at the cat staring back at him. His face paled by at least two shades. "Holy hell, that scared the shit out of me for a minute."

Deke turned his head and grinned. "At least you didn't have nightmares about it chasing you through the jungle." He turned back to the cat. "Damn, I can almost hear the bastard roaring."

"Who painted it?" Gator asked.

"Cassie," Reva replied. "She was up all night doing it."

"Wow." Gator grinned. "Wait till the boys see this. They are gonna seriously freak!"

A loud piercing scream broke the silence a moment later.

Deke, Reva and Gator ran toward the bedroom Cassie was in, not knowing what to expect. They threw the door open and saw her lying on the bed. She was throwing herself this way and that way, struggling against the power of a nightmare.

Deke began to rush toward her when Gator wrapped an arm around his shoulder. "Better call out to her and try to wake her before you touch her. She doesn't look like she's in a good place right now."

Deke nodded as he stared at the pain and agony he saw on her face. Whatever demons she battled in her dreams, they held her close and they were not kind. "Cassie, honey please wake up. It's only a dream." He moved closer while Reva and Gator watched from the doorway. "Come on baby, time to wake up now," he called out a little louder.

His voice must have reached her in her blocked state of mind and she stopped thrashing about. She hadn't opened her eyes yet, but she acted like she could hear him.

"Come on baby, open your eyes and come back to me."

Cassie slowly opened her eyes. At first, she didn't seem to know where she was. Then she turned her head and saw Deke standing there. Her eyes were puffy and her skin was pale. Her nose was runny and blood drained from the corner of her mouth. She leapt at him, wrapping her arms around his neck.

Her tears and sobs wrenched his heart and he could do nothing to help her except hold her. His hands ran up and down her back as he whispered in her ear, "It's okay baby, it's just a bad dream."

~ * * * * ~

Cassie sobbed like her heart was going to break. She was shaking and her arms were trembling with fear. She could taste blood in her mouth but she didn't know why. Deke's arms tightened around her and she didn't care. Here, for just a moment, she felt safe. No one could hurt her as long as he protected her. Then her fears came back. How long would he protect her when he knew the truth? How long would she have a safe haven when he learned all there was to know about her past. She knew he asked Peaches about their past. Peaches would keep her secrets, but could she still be tracked down? Would the police come to arrest her?

Cassie trembled then calmed. She knew she had to find a way to escape again. She couldn't be caught. She had to be free, not locked away in prison. She could never be locked up again. She wouldn't survive this time. If they caught her, it would kill her.

She took a deep breath and raised her head. She glanced toward the door then her face flushed when she saw Reva and Gator standing there.

"Hey." Deke leaned back. "Are you okay now?"

Cassie nodded and wouldn't look at him.

"It was just a bad dream, it can't hurt you," Deke murmured.

"I know. I'm so sorry I caused this much grief," Cassie whispered. "I'm so sorry."

"Hush." Deke's arms tightened around her briefly.

When he let loose, she buried her head in his chest.

"Everyone has bad shit in their past," he said. "Most are lucky enough to leave it there and others dream about it."

"Deke, can I ask you something privately?" she whispered.

Deke looked over at the couple and nodded.

Gator pulled Reva out the door and quietly closed it behind them.

"We're alone now," Deke told her.

Laying her head on his chest, she closed her eyes. She didn't want to see his face when she asked her question. She didn't want to see the horror in his eyes or the revision. "Did you ever hurt someone who really needed hurting? Someone who used pain to control little kids? Someone so vile, he had no soul?"

Deke tightened his hold. "Yes baby, I've hurt someone just like that."

"Did he die because of it?" she whispered.

~* * * *~

Deked raised his head and asked, "Is that what you're so afraid of? That you might have killed somebody who hurt you?"

"I don't think I killed him, I *know* I did. There was just no way he could have lived after the way I hurt him."

Her words were softly whispered, so soft Deke didn't know if he heard her correctly or not. "Honey, I'm not a very good person. I have killed before and will probably do it again, when the time comes. If it comes."

Cassie glanced up at him and frowned. "But I didn't want to kill him. I only wanted to stop him from hurting Peaches."

"Why don't you tell me about it?"

"I can't." She shook her head. "It's not only my secret."

"Sometimes, talking about it helps you cope with the pain. You can't keep that shit inside, it will eat you up."

Cassie laid her head back down on his chest. Closing her eyes, she began telling him about her childhood. At first, the words were halted and faltering. Then as she went on, they became clearer. The hell she described as her life was like a living nightmare he could hardly believe, but he knew it was true. She had been the victim from the time she turned three and she had no one to help her. No one but herself. Then she told him about what happened the night Peaches was attacked. She described in vivid detail what she'd done to a teenage rapist. A boy more than a man but still a vile person. The things she described that this young kid had done to a small child made Deke's blood go cold.

At the age of ten years old, she had saved the life of her best friend by plunging a knife into the body of another human being. A boy four years older than herself and many pounds heavier. She told Deke every detail she had embedded in her brain. The sight of his blood, the smell of the candles he was burning. The taste of his mouth as he tried to kiss her.

Then she showed him her wrists. "Can you still see the rope burns? Mrs. Pierce used to tie me up in the basement for days when she got mad at me." Her words were barely above a whisper now. Her throat was dry and her voice cracked. "I-I can't be restrained and put in a dark basement. I couldn't stand—it. I almost lost my mind being there when I was a kid. I'm afraid of the dark. That's part of why I don't like to be touched. When I was in the dark, all tied up, I felt hands grabbing me, they touched me all over. They pinched me and touched me in places no one should touch. I screamed but no one could hear me. Then the laughter came, driving me further into the blackness. When I got loose that night, my wrists were bloody and so sore I couldn't move them. When I heard Peaches screaming, I ran to her. When I saw the pain and fear on her face, I knew I had to help her. I could barely hang on to anything and Robbie laughed at me. He grabbed the back of my neck and pulled me close to him to kiss me and I wanted to puke. I don't know how I did it but I got the strength to grab a knife and I stabbed him with it. The rage came over me and I kept stabbing him. There was so much blood..."

Deke cradled her head to his chest. "*Shhh*, it's okay. Don't tell me anymore."

Cassie closed her eyes. "But I killed him. I murdered him and I'm so afraid Mrs. Pierce will find me and haul me back to her basement. I'll die down there. I'll die and no one will ever know."

"Honey, I won't let anyone hurt you. I'll kill her first."

"There was only one time I saw her that she acted halfway decent."

Deke ran his fingers along Cassie's back. "Oh, when was that?"

"I guess I was about eight when someone came to the door. I was hiding but I could see her face. When she saw who was there, her face changed. It was as if someone from her past came back and she was happy to see him. I couldn't see him but I could hear the conversation. She called him Calderone and he called her Janie. It didn't make sense to me at the time, but she went with him outside and closed the door behind her. I went to the window and watched them for a few minutes, then he got into his car and he left. She came back into the house and

I hid again. She was wiping tears away and for a moment, she looked upset. Five minutes later, the hellbent old lady I knew so well was back."

"Did this Calderone person ever come back?"

Cassie shook her head and she didn't speak for a few minutes. "Please don't hate me. I'm really not a bad person."

Deke leaned back and holding her face, he kissed her. He thrust his tongue inside her mouth and he kissed her deeply and then he breathlessly pulled his mouth from hers. "Oh baby, I don't hate you. I think I might be falling for you and that scares the hell out of me. I've never loved anyone before."

Cassie threw herself at him. Wrapping her arms around his neck, she kissed him back. When she pulled her mouth from his, she said, "For the first time in my life, I'm not afraid. I know that I'm safe when you hold me. I'm not afraid to let you touch me. I never knew before that a touch could give me this feeling. When you let me kiss you. I'd never known that feeling before. I'm not sure if what I feel for you is love or not, but I want to find out. I think it might be but I'm not sure. I know I don't feel this way for anyone else. I can't stand to think someone else could touch me the way you do."

"No one else will ever touch you the way I do," Deke whispered. "If that happens I'll kill the bastard."

Cassie smiled sadly. "I learned the hard way how to protect myself and Peaches. I learned when someone else hit me, just how much pain I could endure. I learned how to hurt them when they came after me and her...but I hated every minute of it. I just couldn't let anyone else hurt her or me. I just couldn't. She was so scared that night. Robbie cut her bad. She was bleeding so bad, we had to hold up for three days until it stopped. I was so scared, we would get caught."

"I've got you now and I won't let anything or anyone hurt you ever again," Deke vowed.

CHAPTER FOUR

Connie pressed her ear to the door and waited. She'd been lurking in the background waiting for her chance to finally get the dirt on the new bitch and it had paid off. She'd been looking for payback since the fight between them. Wiley had told her not to drag it out, but Connie just couldn't let it go. She'd been waiting and watching over the last few days and keeping track of Cassie's movements. She had to have her revenge. So when she heard that blood curdling scream earlier and the bitch had been sobbing, crying her poor little eyes out, she hid until the coast was clear, Now she was trying to eavesdrop like a little kid.

They were speaking so softly she could barely hear what they had to say. She did hear something about murder though and that made her smile.

"What the fuck do you think you're doing?" Gator roared from behind her.

Connie spun around and was facing a very irate biker.

Gator towered over her on the best of days and this wasn't one of the good days for sure. He grabbed her by the arm and dragged her back to the main room. His steps were so long she couldn't keep up. When he stopped in front of Wiley's table, he tossed her to the floor. "You'd better get your bitch under control, Wiley." Gator snarled. "Deke would not be happy to know she was listening to a private conversation, especially when the conversation is his. In fact, I can damn well guarantee he ain't going to like it."

Wiley got to his feet and stared down at her for a moment.

His face looked blank and Connie knew she wasn't' going to like what happened next. Wiley had told her to drop the anger against Cassie. She hadn't listened and the bitch had beaten her. Wiley told her a second time after the fight to leave it alone and she didn't listen again.

Wiley had been an all right guy, almost perfect for her needs but lately, she felt him pulling away. Connie loved the fact that she was a biker's old lady. She'd thought that over time, she could have it all, a ring, a wedding, kids. Wiley had been good to her, maybe even loved her in his own way.

"Wiley, baby..." she began to plead.

Wiley brought his gaze up to Gator. "Toss the bitch out. She ain't my old lady anymore."

"Wiley—you can't mean that?" Connie screamed. "I know you don't mean it, c-come on baby!"

Wiley grabbed her by the arm and lifted her to her feet. He grasped the back of her vest and yanked it off her shoulders. Then he tossed her to the ground again. Then he sat down to finish his breakfast. He didn't look at her again.

Gator nodded and with a hand motion, two prospects came forward and each one grabbed one of her arms. They half dragged, half carried her to the main door. Connie was sobbing but no one there lifted a finger to help her.

Wiley got to his feet and followed the men. Just before they opened the door, he called out, "Wait a sec, boys."

Connie glanced up at him with hope in her eyes. When he reached into her pocket and pulled out her keys, she thought maybe there was something there to save her. Then he turned and walked away, leaving her and she knew it was over.

The prospects walked her all the way out to the front gate. When it opened, they tossed her out. She stumbled and fell to the dirt. They closed the gate behind her and without a word, they went back to the clubhouse.

Connie lay there in the dirt sobbing. She had just lost everything that ever meant anything to her. She was no longer Wiley's old lady and without him, she knew she'd never be with anyone from the club again. She'd been with Wiley for two years, she'd taken care of him, lived with him, loved him and now she'd lost him. He'd stripped her of more than just her status when he took her vest. Without her keys, she had no place to go, and no car to drive to get her anywhere.

She quickly checked her back pocket and breathed a sigh of relief. At least, she still had her phone. Knowing she might not have it long, she walked down the road and for the first time in her life, she posted club business on the web.

When they had arrived this morning and seen the tiger on the wall of the clubhouse Connie had been stunned.

Everyone had been standing around gazing at the painting. Their remarks had set Connie's teeth off. She hated that Cassie had shown more talent than she ever had in the few days she'd been with them. Knowing it was against the rules, Connie had sneaked a picture of the tiger. The hard and fast rule was, no one spoke about the club and what went on inside the walls. If you broke that rule, you were as good as dead.

Connie turned and glared at the clubhouse, thanks to that little bitch, she was as good as dead to the club anyway. She wasted no time in putting the picture on the web. She even asked the question if anyone out there knew the artist. She couldn't wait to get a response. Carelessly, she tossed the phone into the brush. The phone was under Wiley's name and she knew he would turn it off in a day or so anyway. She couldn't count on him to forget about it.

She wasn't going very far. Connie had one more little trick up her sleeve. She intended to sneak back in when no one else was around and give Cassie one last taste of her revenge. She narrowed her eyes as she remembered Cassie's soft spoken words about being locked up in the dark.

~****~

Deke held Cassie until she'd fallen asleep. Carefully laying her down, he covered her up and leaning over her, he kissed her forehead. He closed the door quietly and glanced at his vice president in surprise. "What the hell are you doing here?"

"We had a problem earlier," Gator growled. "That bitch Connie was listening at the door. I don't know what she heard and it ain't my business to ask but she got an ear full."

Deke's rage at the bitch grew. "Where the hell is she?"

"Wiley stripped her of his cut and tossed her dumb ass out the front door."

Deke thought for a moment then slapped Gator on the shoulder. "You'd better come with me, there's something we need to talk about." He led the way to his office.

While Deke got out a bottle and poured them a drink, Gator shut the door behind them.

Sitting down on the other side of the desk, Deke lifted his glass and toasted, "Hair of the dog." They both slammed the whiskey down and Deke poured another. He sat there thinking for a moment. Finally, he said, "Gator, she told me something about her childhood today. It just about gutted me."

Gator tightened the grip he had on his drink. "You know not every kid has a great time growing up. The world out there can be a harsh place for anybody."

Deke nodded. "But it shouldn't have to be for a little kid. No one should have to be beaten every day from three years old on. Her mom died just before she turned three and her bastard of a father sold her to an evil bitch. He sold his three-year old baby girl."

Gator looked incensed. "Are you fucking kidding me?"

Deke shook his head. "She hasn't told me everything yet, but she will. At least I have a place to start looking." He leaned back and sipped his whiskey. "Peaches told me she met Cassie when they were both five years old and that they both ran away when they were ten. She didn't say why but Cassie told me the story."

"And that was?" Gator asked.

Deke's fingers tightened on his glass. "The bitch's barely teenage son was hurting Peaches. He was cutting her and then he was going to rape her. The bastard was going to rape a ten year old kid."

"How did she get them both the hell away?"

"She heard Peaches screaming and was able to break the ropes they tied her wrists with. Poor kid could barely hold anything in her hands until she saw what the puke was doing to Peaches. She was able to stab the bastard. She said she did it over and over again. She grabbed Peaches and they took off. She said it took three days of hiding to get Peaches in condition to travel and they both have been hiding since then."

"What are you going to do?"

"I'm going to call Rusty and see what he can find out about the attack. She claims she murdered this kid but with everything that went on in that house, any good lawyer would call it self-defense. That little bastard deserved what he got and more."

"Is that why she can't stand to be touched?"

Deke nodded at him. "She told me they would tie her hands together with rope then throw her down in a dark damp basement with no food or water for days. Then they would torment her by grabbing her in all the wrong places. This went on for years and no one would help her."

"Sweet Jesus," Gator whispered. "No wonder being touched freaks her out." He finished his drink. "Where did she learn to defend herself?"

Deke sighed. "She said she learned to take care of herself and Peaches on the street. She said it was tough going for a while but she learned. She would watch from the shadows and learned how to kick box. She said by the time she was twelve, she could take on anyone who messed with them."

"Fuck me," Gator whispered in awe. "Yep, spitfire."

Deke nodded his head in agreement as it was a fitting name...he knew that now. He leaned back and rested his head against the back of his chair. "You know what surprised me the most, Gator?"

"What's that?"

"The other morning I woke up to find her leaning over me. She was looking at me funny and I asked her what she wanted. She told me she'd never kissed anyone before and she asked if she could kiss me."

"And what did you tell her?" Gator smirked.

Deke smiled. "I let her kiss me."

"Of course you did, man." Gator laughed.

"Then I let her do a whole lot more." Deke frowned. "I thought maybe she'd been kidding about never kissing anyone before but I was wrong. The girl was a true innocent."

"A virgin?" Gator asked, astounded.

"Yep, she was and she gave her innocence to me." Deke shook his head. "You know me Gator, I've never had that before. I've always made sure the bitches I fucked knew the score. I've never had anything that sweet before. Never wanted the baggage that goes with a starry eyed girl...but I want this one."

Gator grabbed the bottle and poured them another drink. "Sounds like love, man."

"I know, ain't it a bitch?" Deke slammed his shot down.

"No man, love ain't a bitch," Gator told him quietly. "Love is the best fucking feeling in the world. There ain't nothing finer in the world than the love of a good woman. What Reva and me got, man, I wouldn't trade that for all the gold in the world."

Deke stared at his vice president for a moment then said, "I think I finally found it. With a girl almost half my age."

Gator leaned forward. "I'm gonna let you in on a little known fact. If what you feel for Cassie is real, brother you hang on to that. You fight with every fiber in your body for her, cuz man if she's the one, you'll never have better."

Deke smiled as he remembered the first time they made love. He couldn't begin to describe the feelings he'd had when he took possession of her body. He remembered in vivid details the touch of his lips on hers. He got hard just thinking about her. Adjusting himself, he reached for the phone. "I'd better get Rusty going on this. I want everything I can get."

Gator nodded.

"Maybe we should get Peaches to a safe house," Deke suggested. "With Big Jimmy's death and all this shit, I don't want her out there alone. Cassie would never forgive herself if anything happened to her. They have come too far together for her to lose her friend now."

Gator got up and left the room to take care of business.

Deke tapped Rusty's number and asked him to find out what he could. When he ended the call, he sat there thinking about what he'd learned today. He'd had a bad childhood but it was nothing compared to hers. When he found the club, his life fell into meaning. He had someone strong to stand behind and beside him while Cassie only had Peaches. Together, they had each other and that's all either of them had ever known.

Until now.

Now, they had the club and neither of the girls would ever have to fear the dark again. That he vowed. He would protect them both.

Deke got up and walked out to the main room. He stopped in front of the tiger again, and just stared at the beast. He felt someone come up behind him but he didn't care. Finally, he turned and saw it was Wiley standing there.

"Boss, I'm so sorry for what Connie did this morning. I mean, I can't believe she did it. Well, I can't say that because I know she did it. She's had it in for Cassie ever since you brought her here."

"We both know why she did it. Connie was gonna kick the ass of anyone who hurt you," Deke told him.

Wiley nodded. "But I told her not to do that. Cassie did warn me not to touch her but I thought being bigger, I could take her. Well..." Red color stained Wiley's cheeks. "...I got shown the error of my ways. I mean seriously, that girl's got moves."

Deke felt a bit of pride filling his chest. "On that, I have to agree with you. She can take care of herself."

Wiley turned and gazed at the tiger. "She's got talent too. The patch is great but this tiger? I've never seen anything so real. It almost feels like the damn thing is coming out of the wall, right at you."

"Yeah, it does, doesn't it?" Deke stared at Wiley for a moment then asked, "Are we square on the whole Connie thing?"

"Yeah, boss, we're square." Wiley held out his hand. When Deke shook it Wiley said, "She was getting to be more trouble than pleasure. It would have happened at some not too distant date anyway."

Deke nodded and turned to walk away.

Wiley called out, "Is Cassie going to be okay? We heard her screaming when we came in."

Deke turned to Wiley. "I hope so...I hope so." He continued on his way to the kitchen where Reva was drying a pan. When she looked up at him, he could see concern on her face.

"How is she doing?" Reva asked.

"Better I think." He hesitated then blurted out, "Can you keep an eye on her for me? I know I'm asking a lot but could you just check on her today once or twice, while I'm gone? I need to know she's okay."

Reva smiled and put the pan on the counter. She went to him and wrapped her arms around his waist. "Sure thing hon, I'll watch out for her. If anything happens I'll give you a call."

Deke hugged her tight. "Thanks Reva. You are a good woman. I don't know how you put up with Gator but you deserve better."

Reva laughed. "Honey, what me and Gator have is the best thing that ever happened to me. I don't know what I would do without that man."

"Funny." Deke grinned. "He just told me the same thing about you."

Reva just backed away and smiled. Her cheeks blushed a bright red and she shooed him out the door. "Go to work boss man, go on, get out of here."

"Yes, ma'am." Deke grinned as he turned and left the clubhouse. His spitfire would be in good hands. Swinging his leg over his bike, he started the engine. Revving it, he tore out of the parking lot and headed for the dance club.

~*****~

Deke missed seeing the woman standing behind a tree just outside the main gate. He missed seeing the expression of hate on her face and seeing Connie slip inside the compound, keeping herself in the shadows.

Once she got inside the club, she scurried off to a little used closet to wait for the right time to make her strike. She knew that at some point, everyone would be gone. They all had their own things to do. However, she also knew they would be back, so if she was going to get even with Cassie she wouldn't have long to get the deed done and get out of here in one piece. She realized if anyone caught her back here, she would get beaten or worse, killed for what she was about to do.

When Connie didn't hear any sounds coming from beyond the door of the closet she was hiding in, she opened the door slowly. Peeking around, she found she was alone. She quickly moved toward Deke's bedroom and quietly opened the door. Seeing Cassie asleep, she slipped into the room. Standing next to the bed, she sneered at the other woman. She turned and walked over to one of the shelves in the room and picked up a heavy wrench laying there. She went back to the bed and brought the wrench down on Cassie's head. The sound the impact made was loud and Connie feared someone heard it. She went to the door and peeked out. She was surprised that no one was running toward the bedroom. Then she smiled. No one but her had heard the thud of metal hitting her skull.

She turned back to the girl on the bed. Blood ran from the impact point and was making a stain on the bed sheets but Connie didn't have time to worry about that at the moment. She had to finish her mission and get the hell out of Dodge before anyone caught sight of her.

She grabbed an extension cord and wound it around Cassie's wrists. She made it extra tight, so it would hold her. Then she hoisted the woman over her shoulder and began walking toward the door. Making sure the coast was still clear, she hurried toward the kitchen and beyond.

Opening the basement door, she turned on the lights. Each step she took brought her deeper into the dark dankness below ground. By the time she got to the bottom of the stairs, Connie could see the puddles of water left standing by the recent rains. The dark black mold on the walls stunk to high heaven. Wrinkling her nose at the scent of mold and decay, she carried Cassie's body over to the far corner of the room. The light had shown her there was an anchor embedded in the wall to hold shelving at some point in the past. She looped the end of the cord she'd tied Cassie's hands with and made sure the bindings would hold her.

When she was done, Connie glared at Cassie hanging there in the oblivion of unconsciousness. "You cost me everything I worked for all my life, bitch." Connie sneered at her. Kicking her in the ribs a few times, she said, "The least I can do is repay the favor."

She turned quickly and hurried for the stairway. At the top, she hit the lights and plunged the basement into complete darkness. The last sound in the room was the snap of the door being locked.

Connie then hurried back to the woods before anyone could see her. From there, she began the long walk into town. She would have to find a job and a place to stay. Without any money, it wouldn't be easy. She would have to find a way to get by. She was a survivor.

~* * * *~

Reva smiled as she made her way down the hall to Deke's bedroom. It had been four hours since she checked on Cassie. She knew the other woman needed her sleep but it was time to join the world of the living. She knocked softly on the door and waited for Cassie to call out. When she didn't, Reva knocked a bit harder.

When she didn't hear a sound behind the door, Reva opened it and went inside. When she did, she came to a standstill and felt a horror wash over her. A bloody wrench laid on the floor beside the bed and a small pool of blood stained the sheets. With her body shaking, she wanted to scream but couldn't get any sound to come through her mouth. She turned and ran out to the main room of the clubhouse. Tears flowed down her cheeks as she tried to breathe.

Sobs vibrated from her chest as she stumbled to the kitchen and reached for the phone. Tapping a number she knew by heart, she waited for Gator to pick up the phone.

~* * * *~

Gator was laughing at something Deke had said when his phone rang. The two of them were in the dance hall office. When he answered the call, he could hear someone sobbing. Frowning, he sat up in his chair and held the phone to his ear. "Who is this?"

"Gator, she's gone," his wife cried.

"Who's gone, baby?" Gator asked as fear crawled up his back.

"Cassie. Cassie's gone." Reva sobbed. "I went in to check on her like Deke asked me to do this morning and I found a bloody wrench on the floor and Cassie is missing. Oh, Gator!" she cried out. "There's blood on the sheets."

"We'll be right there baby. Don't worry, we'll find her." Gator ended the call and got to his feet.

Deke stood beside him and asked, "What the fuck is going on, man?"

Gator looked at his brother, his best friend. He didn't know how to tell him, so he just blurted out what he knew, "Your spitfire is missing and there's blood on the sheets."

Deke ran for the door. Gator was right behind him. As they ran through the club, several of the brothers started running as well. They might not know what was going on but when the President and Vice President of the MC start running, they knew enough to rush as well.

Speeding through town, they got to the clubhouse in record time.

Deke didn't even take the time to put his kickstand down. Instead, he handed his bike over to Gator and ran for the door. Throwing it open, he found Reva standing there sobbing.

She was wringing her hands together trying to hold it together.

He grabbed her by her upper arms and looked into her eyes. "What happened?"

"Oh Deke, I'm so sorry!" Reva wailed. "I went to check on her and she was gone."

Deke's fingers tightened on her arms as a crushing fear almost knocked him over.

"Let go of my woman." Growled Gator as he took in the sight of Deke's hands clenching Reva's arms.

Deke snapped his head around to stare at Gator. "What the fuck are you talking about?"

"You're hurting my woman, man." Gator could see the rage on Deke's face and he didn't want Reva on the other end of it.

Deke turned to stare at Reva. He could see the terror and pain on her face. He let go of her arms and pulled her to him. "I never meant to hurt you."

"It's okay, Deke," Reva told him. "I understand but you have to find Cassie. She's hurt and she needs you."

When Deke let her go, Gator grabbed her. "Are you okay, baby?"

Reva shook her head at his concern. Pushing him away, she said, "You go with him. He can't do this alone, honey. He needs you and the boys right now."

Gator kissed her quick and tore down the hall. When he entered Deke's bedroom he found his boss down on his knees. Putting his hand on Deke's shoulders, he gazed at the pool of blood on the bed.

Deke was holding a pillow and it had blood stains on it as well.

Then he looked at the floor. There was a stained wrench sitting there. Gator bent over to pick it up. He could see a fingerprint on the handle. A bloody fingerprint.

Deke looked up at his friend with a lost look on his face. "What the fuck happened, Gator? Where is she?"

Gator frowned. "It looks like somebody snatched her, man." He handed the wrench to his friend.

Deke stared at it. All he could see for a moment was Cassie's blood on the head of the tool. Then he noticed the bloody print. Rage filled him and he threw the weapon into the corner. He got to his feet. "Who would do something like that? Especially here. She thought she was safe here. I told her no one would hurt her, man. Somebody is always around, or they're supposed to be anyway."

"Let's do a search. Whoever took her couldn't have taken her far. The gate stays locked 24/7 man."

Deke and Gator joined the others in the main room. Deke still carried the bloody pillow in his hands. He looked around at all the men standing there. Holding the pillow up, he called out, "My woman is missing and there's blood on the sheets where she was sleeping. I thought our clubhouse was safe for our women and children. This is where we live. This is where we work and play. I want this place searched from top to bottom. I want the parking lot and the woods searched. Don't leave so much as a blade of grass unchecked. We have to find her."

Everyone split up and began searching. They moved furniture out of the corners and checked every room. Some of the guys went outside and began to search the grounds.

Reva joined Deke and Gator. Tears still streamed down her cheeks. "Oh Deke, I'm so sorry, please forgive me."

Deke pulled her in for a hug. "This isn't your fault."

Reva buried her face in his chest. "But she went missing on my watch."

Deke reached down and grabbed her chin bringing it up so she would meet his gaze. "Hey, now, none of that. I asked you to check on her once in a while, I didn't tell you to stand guard. It wasn't on you to protect her; that was on me. I'm the one that failed her. I'm the one that let her be taken. Don't you worry, we'll find her. We have to find her." He brushed her tears away with his thumbs. "Now don't you worry about this. It isn't your fault." He smiled and said, "Go give that man of yours a hug, so he doesn't kill me."

Reva laughed as Gator swept her into his arms and kissed his woman. When he finally pulled away from her, she was blushing bright red. She looked into his adorning eyes and whispered, "I love you big guy."

"I love you too," Gator told her as his big hand patted her ass. "Now, find something to do while we search for Deke's woman."

When Reva left them, Deke gazed down at the pillow in his hands. The pillow still had the scent of her shampoo on it. The amount of blood on it and on his bed told him Cassie was hurt. The question of how badly was what scared him. He could picture her laying in a ditch somewhere bleeding to death and he felt helpless. He glanced over at Gator. "She's out there somewhere alone and scared to death. She's bleeding, man. How can I help her if I don't know where she is? Would she know to come back here if she could or would she crawl into a hole and hide?"

Gator grabbed hold of his friend. "Stop it, man. Get a hold of yourself. It's gonna be okay. You have to believe that. We'll find her. Tell you what, let's get Peaches over here. She knows Cassie the best. She might be able to help and when she finds out Cassie is missing, she'll want to be here anyway."

Deke nodded. "Get her here quickly. We need to find Cassie."

Gator made the call.

Within ten minutes, Peaches was running through the door. "Where is she?" She grabbed Deke's shirt.

"Chill woman, we don't know yet. We're still looking for her."

Peaches let go of his shirt. Her hands clenched into fists and she began pounding on Deke's chest. "You have to find her. You have to!"

Deke grabbed her wrists. "You better calm down, NOW."

Peaches collapsed and would have fallen to the floor in a heap if Deke hadn't caught her. Swinging her up into his arms, he carried her to a table. Calling out for Reva, he set her down. "We'll find her. You have to believe that."

Peaches looked up at him then something caught her eyes. She got to her feet shaking. Her hand went to her mouth and she gasped in shock at the painting on the wall. "Oh, my God..."

Deke got to his feet and stared at Peaches and then the painting. He didn't understand what she was carrying on about. "Cassie painted that last night."

Peaches turned to him. "She did?"

Deke nodded. "What does it mean to you?"

"Cassie paints when she wants to share a little something of herself with you. She has talent but she's very careful just who she shares it with. It's her own secret." She turned to study the tiger again. "This is Rufus. She named him that the first and only other time she drew him. He became her escape route when the old battle axe would hurt her. When she would be lying there all curled up in a ball after a beating, she wouldn't be crying her little heart out. She would be talking to

Rufus. She would be hurting so bad but she never shed a tear." Peaches shook her head. "Not Cassie. She'd never let it out that she was in pain because she didn't want Mrs. Pierce to know she'd broken her. Cassie wouldn't give her the satisfaction."

Deke stared at the painting of the tiger. "So, what does it mean for her to have painted this here?"

Peaches moved closer and reached out a hand to touch Rufus. "She's sharing her most intimate feelings with you. She's sharing her art. It's the one thing in her life she could really call her own and she swore no one would ever take it away from her. In other words, she's sharing herself with you and your club." She stared at the painting again. "Isn't he beautiful?" she whispered.

"You said she drew him one other time. When and where was that?"

Peaches frowned. "She drew him on the walls in Mrs. Pierce's basement where she was tied up all the time. She told me it was the only thing she could do to keep her sanity. She scratched him out of the stone wall with a rock."

Deke felt like he'd been punched in the gut as it occurred to him. He turned to Gator and asked, "Does this place even have a basement?'

Gator shrugged. "Damned if I know."

They both turned to Reva.

She was nodding. "Yeah, it does but it's nasty down there, so we don't use it." She got to her feet and walked over to the door leading to the basement. Everyone had followed her through the kitchen. When she reached for the handle, she felt the resistance. Reva frowned and looked at Gator. "This door wasn't locked earlier today."

"How do you know that?" Deke asked.

"I went down there early this morning, thinking we could clean it up and start using it again, but I found standing water on the floor and black mold three feet up the walls. I was going to say something to you guys but it slipped my mind."

Deke moved her out of the way and checked the lock on the door. What he found wasn't good. He glanced over his shoulder at Gator. "Somebody broke off something inside the lock. We're going to have to break the door to get down there."

"I'll go find a crowbar," Gator told him.

Reva backed away from the door. She looked over at Peaches then grabbed her by the hand and pulled her into the main room. Sitting her down at one of the tables, she picked a bottle from behind the bar. She poured the girl a drink and shoved it into her hands. "Drink."

Peaches shook her head. "Don't drink. Me and Cassie have never touched booze and we vowed we never would."

"Drink it," Reva repeated.

Peaches frowned. "No, I won't do it. Me and Cassie made a vow. I'm not breaking it."

Reva slammed the drink down her throat and waited while the liquor burned its way to her belly. One by one, the other members trickled back to the clubhouse. She could see by the defeated look on their faces...they hadn't found anything.

The sounds of splintering wood came from the kitchen area and everyone stood still, waiting. They heard the sounds of heavy boots descending the basement stairs and then they all heard a male cry of anguish echoing through the clubhouse. Everyone looked at each other. It was a sound they'd never heard before and never wanted to hear again.

~****~

Cassie groaned as she came back from oblivion. Her head ached and her wrists hurt. She tried to struggle but her hands wouldn't move. She could feel the bite of the restraints get tighter and it lent to her struggle with the past. The smell of mold hit her and her mind flashed back to when she was a child. She didn't want to open her eyes. She didn't want to find out if she was back in her own little corner of hell. She tried to move her wrists but couldn't. The reality of where she was came down on her. She had escaped this particular hell at one of the lowest points in her life and now, she knew even without seeing it with her own eyes—she was back.

She started to remember the days when she was trapped down here as a child. Her body remembered the beatings she took. She could still feel the strap as it burned her tiny body after each and every stroke.

Cassie finally opened her eyes and saw nothing. She wanted to scream but couldn't. Her throat wouldn't allow any sound to be released. Her own fears wouldn't allow any sound to penetrate the darkness that surrounded her. It wouldn't allow her to struggle against the obvious but it would allow her to surrender herself to the past.

With her eyes wide open, Cassie sank down into her own hell as the past came back and took over. She was too tired to fight it, so she didn't. She gave up the struggle to survive and she let the fears take her.

~****~

Deke flipped the lights on and came down the steps. When he saw her hanging there, eyes wide open staring at nothing, he let out a cry of anguish. He rushed to her side and carefully picked her up in his arms. Gator reached out with his pocketknife and cut the cord that bound her to the wall.

Neither man spoke as the made their way back to the stairs leading back to daylight.

Slow heavy steps came back up the stairs. Gator came out first leading the way. Deke carried Cassie in his arms. Without a word to the men standing there, he made his way down the hall to his bedroom where he carefully laid Cassie down. Gator, Reav and Peaches followed him but everyone else stayed behind.

A moment later, Reva came out of the bathroom with a basin of water and a cloth to bathe the wound on her head.

Deke took the rag away from her and knelt beside the bed. Dunking the cloth in the water, he cleaned the wound on her head.

Her eyes still stared at nothing and she was acting like she couldn't hear him calling her to come back to him.

Peaches was on the other side of the bed sobbing.

Deke couldn't make her leave. Cassie might be his woman but she was also Peaches' best friend. If he couldn't find a way to bring her back maybe Peaches could.

Deke looked down at her hands. Whoever had done this had wrapped a cord tightly around her wrists. Her poor hands were turning blue due to lack of circulation. He tried to unravel it but it was just too damn tight. Suddenly, there was a knife being held out to him and Deke took it. Looking up he saw Gator standing beside him. Deke nodded and began cutting the cord.

When the last little bit of the cord holding her hands together snapped, her wrists fell to the bed with a plop. Deke grabbed one wrist and began rubbing life back into it.

Peaches grabbed the other one and did the same. "Oh Cassie, please come back. I know you can hear me. Please come back to me sweetie. I need you in my life again. I can't make it on my own without you." She sobbed. "I need you baby girl. It's supposed to be you and me against the rest of the whole damn world. Please come back."

The coloring in her hands was returning to normal but Cassie was still staring into nothing. There was no sign of life. Her heart was beating but she was caught up in her nightmare.

"Cassie, baby, you need to listen to me, " Deke whispered. "I need you to come back here. I love you baby."

Cassie's finger slowly curled around his hand. Her eyes were still blank but it was a sign.

Gator tapped him on the shoulder and motioned for him to come outside.

When he moved out, Reva took his place. With her and Peaches, at least Cassie wouldn't be alone while he was gone. He hated to leave her but he had business to take care of. Closing the door behind them, Deke asked, "What did they find?"

When they entered the main room everyone was silent for a moment then Wiley stepped forward and handed him a phone.

Deke glanced up at Wiley.

"It's Connie's phone."

"What does this have to do with anything?" Deke asked.

"I took her property vest back after she was caught listening at your door this morning," Wiley explained. "I took her keys but forgot about the cell. One of the Prospects found it outside the gates on the search today. This would be something she would do to get me back. Either that or to get even with Cassie."

Deke's fingers tightened on the phone.

"There's something else you should know, boss." Wiley straightened his shoulders.

"What would that be?' Deke asked.

"She broke the rule."

"What rule would that be?"

"I checked on her last message. She put a photo of the tiger out on the web and asked anyone and his brother if they knew anything about it. She also put our name out there. Everyone knows where the painting is at."

Deke's fingers broke the phone in half. The first rule of any MC club was not to talk about what happens inside the clubhouse. To do so meant death. Everybody knew this and everyone abided by this rule. He looked over at his Sergeant at Arms. "You know what to do. Don't kill her on the outside, bring her stupid ass back here, I want her to admit what she did before she dies."

Wiley nodded. He tightened his lips and turned toward the door.

Three others fell in line behind him and the four men left the building.

Deke turned and returned to his bedroom. Closing the door behind him, he reached for the closest bottle. Chugging the liquor down, he waited for the familiar burn.

CHAPTER FIVE

When Deke's phone rang a couple of hours later, he almost ignored it. But it kept ringing. Hauling it out of his pocket he growled, "What the fuck do you want?"

"Just giving you a head's up." Rusty's voice came over the line.

"About what?"

"The picture of the tiger went viral," Rusty explained. "When it hit the net this morning along with your address, several agencies suddenly became very interested."

"Who and why?"

"Boston police Detective Lance Sullivan for one. Seems the man has an open murder case sitting on his desk. Boston Child Services for another. They seem to have misplaced two wards of the state several years ago."

"Anybody else I need to know about?" Deke asked drily.

"Yeah." Rusty paused. "Mrs. Eleonore Pierce wants to know the whereabouts of the two missing girls. She's even offering a reward of a hundred thousand dollars for information and, or their return. From what I can understand, she doesn't care in what condition they are returned in as long as both girls are still breathing."

"What the fuck is her interest?"

"One of the girls she claims killed her son, Robbie."

"How did she know?"

"The painting resembles something the girl did on her basement wall."

Deke sighed heavily. "So, what I asked you to find out this morning is really true?"

"Yeah, every fucking word. The cops are closing in on the girls, and Mrs. Pierce has the clout to make sure they never see the light of day again."

"Did she kill Robbie the night of the attack?"

"No he lived, but the girl did a number on his manhood. It seems he felt life wasn't worth living without his dick. He blew his brains out three weeks later. Got his hands on daddy's gun and pulled the trigger with his own little hand."

"Fuck a duck," Deke whispered.

"Yeah and Mama's had eleven years to wait for her revenge. That woman is a bitch of the worst kind."

"Okay, let me know whatever else you can find out. We're going on lockdown once we settle the business of the leak."

"Are you all right, man?" Rusty asked. "You sound a little strange."

"Yeah, there's been some goings on here. That bitch Connie was caught snooping at my door. Wiley took her cut and tossed her sorry ass out. Then she leaked that picture and our MC over the net, clocked Cassie in the head and put her down in the basement. It wasn't good."

"Poor girl." Rusty cleared his throat. "I'll try to let you know when the cops are on their way down to you."

"Thanks, I appreciate it." Deke ended the call and got to his feet. He'd been sitting in the bedroom all afternoon. It was time to take care of business. He glanced over at Peaches. She was curled up on the bed with Cassie and both of them were sleeping.

He left the bedroom quietly. His footsteps echoed as he moved down the hall. When he got to the main room, everyone was looking for word of how Cassie was doing. He went over to Gator's table and sat down. Deke ran his fingers over his tired face. "She and Peaches are sleeping. I don't think she's back yet, at least not all the way. She's fighting some pretty bad demons."

Reaching over, Reva patted his hand. "At least she's trying."

Deke nodded, then looked over at Gator. "Are the boys back yet?"

Just then, they all heard the roar of motorcycles pulling into the parking lot. They waited for Wiley and the others to come in.

Everyone could hear a woman screaming, begging for her life, as they got closer to the door. Wiley dragged Connie into the room by her hair. He had to pull her along and he wasn't gentle about it. He brought her over to where Deke and Gator were sitting, then threw her on the floor.

Connie was crying and screaming at the whole bunch of them, then she peered up at Deke as she paled and shut her mouth.

Deke picked up his drink and sipped it. "I just got a phone call from Rusty. He told me that someone posted a photo this morning on the World Wide Web. It was a photo of Cassie's painting. Peaches told me earlier that Cassie doesn't share her art with anyone until she feels safe. In fact, Peaches was very surprised when she saw old Rufus here." He grinned and motioned to the tiger on the wall. "Peaches told me that when Cassie had nobody else to talk to, she could always talk to Rufus."

Connie looked perplexed and terrified. They all knew this tone. The way he spoke and the way he smiled. It meant hell was coming and Deke would be serving up cold justice.

He turned back to the group. "We have been betrayed, my brothers. Connie betrayed us to the whole world when she posted that picture. Now, we have badges coming our way. Johnny Law is coming all the way from Boston after my woman and they know right where to come, thanks to Connie."

The room went silent except for Connie's whimpering.

Deke slammed down another shot of whiskey. "I know all of you have had a hard life. It isn't easy for any of us to grow up. Hell, the only family I ever had was either in the service or here with you all. But I'll tell you a little bit of Cassie and Peaches' story, so you can understand the hell they went through. At the age of three, Cassie lost her mother. Her father sold her to Mrs. Eleonore Pierce. Pierce used her as a slave and used to beat the shit out of her on a regular basis. Cassie stood up for every other kid in that house and got beat down for her troubles. Pierce threw her tiny little body in a dark basement, after she beat the hell out of her, for days at a time, just for kicks. She left her tied up all alone for days. That's what Connie overheard this morning. When we all left to do our normal business, Connie came back. She hit Cassie on the head with a fucking wrench, while she was sleeping, tied her up and left her to die in our basement."

When Deke stopped talking the room was silent as all the members stared at the woman on the floor in disgust.

Connie hung her head down and was still crying.

Deke searched the faces of each of his men. "I know life isn't fair but for a ten year old kid, there should be something more than what she had. One night when she heard Peaches screaming she busted out and went to find her only friend. She saw Robbie Pierce, a fourteen year old pig cutting and trying to rape a ten year old little girl. She didn't manage to kill him, the bastard took his own life three weeks after the fact. But she did almost cut off his dick. They managed to escape and have been living on the streets since then. Now thanks to this bitch, old lady Pierce has a bounty on my woman and the badges are coming here."

"What do you want us to do boss?" Wiley asked.

"Two things...The first thing, you have to seal *her* fate." Deke nodded his head at Connie. "You all have to pronounce what's going to happen to her, then you have to decide if you think I'm still your President. You all may think my feelings for this woman have led me astray. And you may all be right. I will use everything I can to protect her but I won't use this club, if you guys aren't comfortable with it. I can't betray everything this club stands for, for my own personal gain. I won't do that to you guys. I love and respect you guys too much for that." Deke sat down and poured himself another drink.

No one said a word. Finally, one by one they all came forward and stood behind Deke. The last one standing there was Wiley. He went to stand behind Connie. Before she could raise her head, he grabbed her by the hair and pulled her head back. Then while staring into Deke's eyes he took his knife and slit her throat. Blood sprayed everywhere.

Wiley threw her body to the ground. Then he laid the bloody knife on the table and joined his brothers standing behind Deke.

Everyone was waiting for him to speak when they heard footsteps coming from the back hall. Deke stood and turned to see Peaches helping Cassie coming toward him. She still looked incredibly weak but with Peaches' help, they made their way to within a few feet of where Deke sat. Everyone moved to make a path.

A few of the men stepped in front of Connie's body. They all watched as Peaches let Cassie go.

She took a few steps to come to a halt in front of him. Without saying a word, she reached up and wrapped her arms around his neck. When her lips touched his, Deke grabbed her to him and kissed her for all she was worth. Everyone cheered and Deke could feel tears rolling down her face. He could taste them but he didn't care.

Cassie leaned away from his embrace for a moment. "I'm sorry I left you for a while."

"You came back to me." Deke smiled. "That's all I care about. You came back."

"It was hard to do," she whispered. "I almost didn't. I almost stayed in the shadows. It's easier to do."

Deke sat down and hauled her into his lap. Several of the guys dragged Connie's body out the back door and the women got busy cleaning up the blood. Deke held Cassie's face to his chest until everything was done. He didn't want her to see any of it. Then he let her go.

Peaches, Reva and Gator sat down with them.

Finally, Cassie spoke up, "I know its club business and I have no right to ask, but Peaches and I heard some of what you said. Can you tell me what's going on?"

Deke reached for his drink. After swallowing it, he told her, "Connie betrayed both you and the club. She was listening at the door this morning and heard everything you told me. She's the one who hit you and took you to the basement. She brought the police, Boston Child Services and Mrs. Pierce down on us." Then he shrugged. "She paid for her betrayal." He tilted her chin up to look into her eyes. "Life is hard in a MC. She knew the rules, the same as everybody else here does."

Cassie nodded. "Those are the same rules all over, even on the streets. You rat out your friends and you pay for it with your life." Then she shuddered. "I do wish she hadn't included Mrs. Pierce though. She's a stone cold bitch."

"That bitch has a hundred thousand dollar bounty on your head," Deke told her.

Cassie paled.

"What?' Peaches yelled. "That's just wrong."

Cassie shook her head. "I killed Robbie. She thinks she's justified."

"But you didn't kill the little puke. You just cut off his dick. He blew his own brains out three weeks after your attack."

Cassie shrugged. "I was still behind what he did. She won't care that he pulled the trigger with his own filthy hands."

"We aren't giving you up, Spitfire," Wiley called out. "We stand behind our President and will protect you from both the law and this Pierce bitch."

Cassie paused at the nickname then she blushed and smiled. Looking around she said, "Thank you. As for the law and Child Services, I have evidence of the horrors that went on in that house. I'd been collecting it for some time before Peaches and I left. Before we got out, I took her scrapbook. She has pictures of what happened to the kids there. I took it all and hid it."

"Can you get it here?" Gator asked. "That would clear your name for the police."

"It's out in the door panel of my Jeep. I've carried that stuff for too long already. You learn early in life not to trust anyone but yourself. It has to be that way sometimes."

Deke looked at his men. "We go to lock down. No one in or out, for however long it takes. One badge in particular, Lance Sullivan is heading here. I want a roaming watch until they get here." He looked over at Gator. "Get rid of Connie's body where no one will ever find it. I don't want that coming back to us."

"We'll take her over to the pig farmer."

"Do it now and when you get back, we'll lock it down. I want an armed guard standing watch. I'm not taking any chances someone will jump the fence and come after her. A hundred grand is a lot of money."

Gator got up and three guys followed him out the back door.

Cassie sighed. "Maybe Peaches and I should just leave."

Deke held her tighter. "You girls aren't going anywhere. I'm not letting you go. If you really have the evidence you say you do, then the law isn't going to have a case against you. If I need to handle this Pierce woman I will." Deke scowled. "She's gonna wish she'd never been born if I go after her." He patted her thigh. "Let's go see what this evidence of yours looks like. I like to know exactly where I stand."

Together, they walked out to her Jeep and she showed him her secret hiding place. It was very hard for her to turn it over but she did. She watched him take the packet, her eyes glued to the envelope.

Deke lifted her face to his. "Are you sure you can do this?"

"What do you mean?" Cassie frowned.

"You can't take your eyes off of this. Don't you trust me with it?"

"Yes. I do trust you with it but you have to understand that for half my life, I've been protecting those papers. It's very hard to turn them over to anyone. I don't trust easily and if anyone but you had asked me for it, I wouldn't have turned it over. My life and Peaches' depends on that evidence. Without it, I would go to prison or worse, Eleonore Pierce could get her hands on us. This isn't just my life at stake, it's Peaches' life too. I have to protect her."

Deke leaned forward and laid his forehead on hers. "Sweetheart, that's my job now. To protect both you and Peaches. If you let me, I promise I won't let you down. I'd give my life for yours."

Cassie smiled. "I don't want your life given for mine. I want to share whatever life I have with you. I know we haven't known each other very long but I have to believe you came into my life for a purpose. I want to make love to you again and again, for the rest of my life. Please understand I've never known love before. I've never had to share my feelings with anyone but Peaches before. I might make some mistakes or screw this whole thing up. I hope I don't, but I might. Please give me a chance and don't hold my mistakes against me."

"I'll do whatever I have to, to keep you. You have to trust me on this." She held out her small hand.

"I do trust you." He took it into his large one and they went back inside the clubhouse together.

When they sat down again, Deke spread the evidence on the table. He and Gator began going through what was there.

Cassie felt a little embarrassed by what was there but Deke and Gator didn't look like they thought any less of her because of what they read.

She and Peaches went to the kitchen to make coffee. While they were there, Reva joined them. "How are you doin, girls?"

Cassie smiled. "I haven't quite recovered but I'm getting there. My head hurts. I still feel a little shaky and the nightmare isn't quite pushed all the way to the back of my mind."

"Yeah, I can see that." She shook her head. "I still can't believe Connie did that. I'll give you some aspirin. I was glad to see it wasn't as bad as I thought with all that blood."

"I'm sorry about it all too. I really don't like to be touched. I told Wiley that several times and when he grabbed me, I lost it. I didn't mean to hurt him."

Reva snorted. "He should have listened and learned the first time, the dumb ox. The second inning was his own damn fault, and he knew it. She should have left it alone, but she didn't. In this life, you do whatever your man tells you or you suffer the consequences. She's also been here long enough to know you don't rat out the club. She put not only your life in danger but everyone who calls this place home. She knew that, yet did it anyway."

Peaches shuddered. "Cassie has always been tougher than me. She's been the one all this time to watch over me and I'm very grateful she's always had my back. Even when I was snatched she was brave enough to come looking for me."

Cassie smiled. "We're sisters from different parents' girl, I told you that a long time ago. I'll always have your back but hey, you aren't the only one getting something out of this relationship. You've given me back something too."

Peaches wrapped her arms around Cassie and held her tight.

Deke popped his head into the kitchen. "Cassie, Peaches... we need to talk to you two for a minute. Can you come out here?"

Cassie searched his face but she couldn't read his expression. Grabbing Peaches' hand, they walked out to the main room. They went over to the table and Cassie gasped as she saw the pictures spread out on the wooden surface. Tears welled in her eyes and she grabbed Peaches' hand a bit tighter.

"What's going on in these pictures?" Deke asked. "Who is this little girl?"

The pictures in question showed a little girl laying on her stomach. Her back and legs had been whipped and she had several open wounds. Wounds that oozed blood. It ran down her back and legs.

Cassie sat down on a chair and stared at the pictures. She remembered that day very clearly.

"Oh Cassie," Peaches sobbed. "You have to tell them."

Cassie shook her head violently. "I can't tell anyone what happened that day. I'm too ashamed."

Deke knelt beside her chair. "You don't need to be ashamed, but sweetheart I need to know. Is this little girl you?"

After a long moment, Cassie nodded. "Yes, that's me but I can't talk about that day." She sobbed. She got up and ran down the hall. They all heard the door slam shut and her sobs long after it closed.

Deke looked over to Peaches.

Tears rolled down her cheeks. She too, sat down, laid her head on her arms and sobbed. A few minutes later, she stopped. Raising her head, she wiped her tears away and began to talk, "That was the day Mrs. Pierce came the closest to breaking Cassie." Her words were barely more than a whisper but everyone standing around could hear them. "The old bitch had picked a fight with one of the small kids because she knew Cassie would watch out for them, she always did. She used to tell us that somebody had to fight for the little ones and Cassie was always sticking up for someone. Anyway, that day was the worst day. Mrs. Pierce almost killed her." She took a deep breath, let it out and went on with her story, "That day Willie had dropped his glass of milk. Cassie was on the floor cleaning up the mess and Mrs. Pierce grabbed her belt and began beating her with it. She was screaming the whole time about how ungrateful she was that somebody had opened her home to kids nobody else wanted." Peaches halted and swiped at a tear on her cheek.

Everyone waited for her to continue.

"Cassie made the mistake of telling the old bitch she may be unwanted but she was still a person and she had rights. The old lady lost it then. She ripped Cassie's shirt off and beat the hell out of her. It never got as bad as it did that day. She was covered in blood but the old bat wouldn't stop. She hauled Cassie down to the basement and tied her to the wall. Then she set Robbie down there to teach her a lesson. We could hear Cassie screaming and when she stopped, Robbie came back up. He told his mother she had learned a good lesson. That was the day Cassie drew Rufus. That was the time she was alone in the dark for four days. They didn't feed her or even give her any water. When they brought her back upstairs, Cassie had a certain look in her eyes and she couldn't stand to be touched. That was a week before we left."

"Did she ever tell you what the little bastard did to her?" Deke asked. "He didn't rape her, she was a virgin."

Peaches looked at him sadly. "She didn't have to tell me what Robbie did to her." She shuddered. "Robbie always was a pervert that way. He loved dishing out pain."

Deke closed his eyes when he understood what happened that day. "I think it's a good thing Robbie is gone. I'd have a hard time with him still breathing."

Gator laid his hand on Deke's shoulder.

Deke got to his feet and walked down the hall. Opening the door, he slipped inside and closed the door behind him.

Cassie was curled up on the bed.

When he went over to the bed and sat down, she moved away.

Deke pulled her close to him. "I'm so sorry honey."

"How can you stand being close to me now?" she finally asked. "I'm damaged goods."

Deke tightened his hold on her. "No baby, you're not. Robbie was one sick mother fucker and what he did to you and the other kids in his mother's charge wasn't right. The fact his own mother allowed him to do it doesn't say much about her. She's the one who needs to go to jail. The bitches in the joint will teach her right and wrong. I guarantee that."

"But I'm dirty, I feel so dirty."

"No you aren't." Deke insisted. "Anal sex can be pleasurable when it's done right. Robbie didn't do it with pleasure in mind, he used pain as a weapon, a tool and he was a sick fuck."

Cassie was still for a moment then she turned to look at him. "Have you ever—you know..."

Deke grinned softly. "Yeah baby, I have but my partner enjoyed herself. I didn't hurt her." He hesitated then told her, "I enjoyed it too."

"Can we have sex again? I want to feel something other than being so lost. I want to feel alive again and that's what I feel when you're inside me," Cassie whispered. "I need to feel alive."

Deke was still awed by her innocence and her forthright ways. When she wanted something, she simply asked for it. He smiled as he stood up.

Cassie sat there and watched as he pulled off his shirt and jeans.

When he was naked, he reached for her clothes. A few minutes later, he joined her on the bed. Deke leaned toward her and began kissing her. When she opened her mouth to his, he plunged his tongue in deep.

Cassie groaned. She wrapped arms around his neck and pulled him closer.

Deke's hands made their way to her breasts and he rubbed his thumbs over her hard nipples.

Cassie could feel her body responding. Her pussy was getting wet and she needed his cock inside her. Pulling him down on top of her, she opened her legs and arched her hips. "For so long, I've felt nothing and I was okay with that. Nothing was worse than the pain, but you've shown me something so new and I want to feel it again." She shook her head. "I *need* to feel it again..."

~*****~

Deke felt his cock throb at her words. Without thinking, he thrust hard and deep inside her. He felt the walls of her pussy wrapping around him. She felt so good, so tight, so wet. Pulling back, he plunged even deeper. Several thrusts later, he could feel his body tighten. He knew he couldn't hold out too much longer. "Cassie, I need you to come," he whispered. "I'm so close."

Cassie arched her back as her entire body quaked.

He groaned as he ground his hips against hers and came inside her. Sweat dripped down Deke's temple as he leaned forward covered her mouth with his. His tongue thrust into her mouth and she met his invasion with one of her own. Finally, he rolled off and plopped down on the bed beside her. Wrapping his arms around her, he pulled her to his side.

Cassie let him hold her but only for a moment. When she pulled away, she wrapped her shoulders in the blanket.

She leaned back into his arms again, but it didn't feel the same to Deke. He wanted her warm body naked, not draped in a blanket.

Cassie touched his chest lightly with the tips of her fingers. "I never knew it could be like this."

He squeezed her tighter to him.

"So, when do you think they will come?"

Deke sighed. "I don't know but we have to get ready. We aren't that far from Boston, so they could be here anytime."

Cassie nodded. "I suppose we'd better get dressed then, huh?"

Deke rolled to a sitting position and grabbed his pants. Standing up, he reached for his shirt, he pulled it over his head and sat down to put on his boots. Cassie hadn't moved and he turned his head to see her watching him. When she didn't say anything, he got up and went to the door. With one last look at her, he went back to the main room. She wore an odd expression. He wondered what she was thinking. It could just be all that she was going through, but he felt there was more she wasn't telling him.

When he reached the table where Reva and Peaches sat, he joined them. Pouring himself a drink, he glared over the rim of his glass at Peaches. "What else do I need to know before this shit hits the fan?"

CHAPTER SIX

Peaches paled and shook her head. "You know everything now. When she gave you the evidence we carried away that night...that was everything."

"Why do I doubt that?" Deke stared at her.

Peaches studied the tiger painting on the wall for a moment. "I'm surprised she handed it over to you actually."

"Why?" Deke took a sip of his drink.

Peaches turned to study him now. "You don't know the hell we went through. Cassie had been gathering that evidence for weeks before we left. She wouldn't even tell me where she kept it. Even after we left, she would hide it. I asked her where and she would never tell me. All she ever said was that it was safe and as long as we had it, we were safe."

Before he could respond, the main door flew open. Gator and the men he'd taken with him to dispose of Connie's body returned.

Gator joined them and Reva poured him a drink.

"Did everything go okay?" Deke asked.

Gator nodded over the top of his glass. "That old sow made little work of her."

"Did you have any problems coming back?"

Gator shook his head.

"How was traffic?" Deke asked.

Gator stared at him as if he wanted to say something but couldn't. "Lots of traffic out there, more than usual anyway."

Deke nodded. "We'd better get locked down then. Make sure the guys standing watch do their jobs. I don't want any surprises."'

Gator got to his feet and walked to the door. Some of the men sitting around joined him and they went outside.

Reva pushed herself away from the table. "I suppose I'd better get a meal together."

"Just make sandwiches or something simple. The guys will be coming and going all night. Make sure you have plenty of coffee going. I don't want anyone drinking too heavily until this is over," Deke ordered.

Reva smiled slightly. "You got it boss."

That left Peaches sitting with Deke. After a minute or so, she began to fidget. "I'd better go help Reva." She got to her feet.

"Sit down," Deke ordered without looking at her.

Peaches sat down hard.

"So, tell me what happened after you two left the Pierce household."

Peaches' hands began to shake and she wrapped them around her empty glass to hold it together. She couldn't look at him and she had no idea what he wanted to know. "We left, we survived, and we made a new life for ourselves. What more is there to say?"

Deke glared at her but before he could say anything, he heard Cassie behind him.

"Why don't you ask me what you want to know?"

Turning his head, he found her standing there.

~*****~

"Why do you have to sneak around behind my back? My secrets don't mean a damn thing to you do they?"

Peaches got to her feet. Her face was pale and she looked like she was going to cry. "Cassie, I wasn't gonna tell him, I promise." With a cry, she turned and ran to the kitchen.

"What are you hiding from me?" Deke demanded.

"Not a fucking thing you need to know." Her voice was flat and sarcastic. "I don't owe you a damn thing. If you don't want me here, I'm gone. In fact, maybe I should just leave, that way whoever is coming will just go away. They can chase after me and you and your fucking club won't have to worry."

Earlier, when the door had closed behind him and she sat in his bedroom, Cassie felt tears rolling down her cheeks. She didn't know why she cried. She didn't know anything about sex before she met him but she knew he wasn't giving her everything. She didn't expect him to love her, hell she didn't know what love was. So maybe she was wrong about him holding back but somehow deep down inside, she didn't think so.

"You aren't leaving here!" Deke yelled.

"You can't fucking keep me here!" Cassie yelled back.

"The hell I can't." Deke growled.

"Go to hell." Cassie snarled. Before he could respond, she swept the evidence together and stomped off toward the kitchen.

Reva didn't look up at her, instead she ignored her altogether. She kept her hands busy making sandwiches.

Cassie searched the kitchen for her friend. She found Peaches sitting in the corner sobbing. She went over and sat down beside her. She wrapped her arm around the other woman's shoulder and held her tight while Peaches cried. Cassie stared straight ahead. Tears burned her eyes but she wouldn't cry. She wouldn't give Deke the satisfaction of making her cry.

Peaches sobs lessened and finally stopped. Cassie knew she had fallen asleep and that was fine with her. She didn't want to talk. The pain was too great and she thought her world would shatter any minute. She was barely holding on and right now, she needed room to breathe.

When Reva returned, she came over to where the girls were sitting. Without saying anything, she spread a blanket over both of them. Then she left them alone.

~****~

Deke sat there fuming. He'd never felt a rage quite like the one he was feeling now. He didn't know how she did it. How she knew just what to say to make him flip. She was so damn stubborn, he wanted to spank her. Every little detail of her life was a battle to get her to share. She had too many secrets and he wanted to know them all, but he wanted her to share them with him. He didn't want to have to ask about them. He swallowed his whiskey but before he could pour another, the door opened and Gator walked in. "Is everything set?"

Gator nodded. "Yup, but just as we locked the gate a car drove up. Detective Lance Sullivan wants a sit down."

Deke sighed. "First, tell Reva the girls need to stay in the kitchen till he's gone. Then let him in but only him. Nobody else is welcome. Also, make sure he gives up his gun. If he really wants answers, he'll cooperate."

Gator nodded and headed to the kitchen then after a moment, he went back outside.

Deke filled his glass and waited. When the door opened, he turned and saw Detective Sullivan coming his way. Deke waited until both men joined him. Gator sat down and they waited until Detective Sullivan sat across from him.

"So, what can I do for the Boston police?" Deke drawled.

Sullivan turned his head and studied the tiger on the wall. "So that's what he should look like." Turning back to Deke, he cleared his throat and said, "I'm looking for two young women."

Deke snorted. "Good luck with that, man. What makes you think they're here? We aren't exactly known for entertaining young women."

Sullivan opened the file folder he'd brought with him and took out a black and white photo. He slid it across the table in front of Deke.

Deke glanced at it and saw the outline of a tiger etched on a stone wall. The lines were crude and uneven, as was the surface of the wall they were drawn on. He studied the drawing then turned to view the painting on his wall. They were one and the same. He shrugged and pushed the photo back to Lance. "What makes you think she's still here?"

"This is the closest I've gotten in over eleven years to finding them. I had to come." Sullivan shrugged. "When this case hit my desk eleven years ago…I thought all it would take was time to find them, but that was my mistake. I couldn't believe we'd have any trouble finding a couple of kids." He shook his head. "The longer the case sat there unsolved, the more it bothered me."

"What does that mean?" Gator asked gruffly.

"I met Mrs. Eleonore Pierce when I got a call about an attack on a fourteen year old boy. Robbie Pierce had been attacked inside his own home. The injuries he had I wouldn't wish on my worst enemy. While he was in surgery, I tried to get a statement from his mother but she was in no condition to give one."

"She was that upset?" Deke frowned.

"She wasn't upset as much as she was enraged. Mrs. Pierce ran a fourteen bed state funded home for foster kids. She lived on site with her husband and teenage son. The whole time I was there, she kept pacing back and forth talking to herself. I stayed long enough to find out how Robbie was, then left. The next morning Mrs. Pierce came to the precinct to file charges against the girls. She demanded they be found and attempted murder charges be put on one of the girls." Sullivan narrowed his eyes and stared at Deke as if to judge his reaction.

Deke shrugged. "What are these dangerous girls' names? If I run into them I'll give you a call."

"They're names are Josette Rearden and Callie Blake."

Deke nodded and kept his expression blank. "If I run into them, I'll let them know to call you." He picked up his drink and sipped it.

Sullivan stood but didn't walk away. Instead, he said, "I know there's more to the story than I've been told. Mrs. Pierce isn't going to give up and every year she comes to see me. She demands to know what progress is being made on finding the woman who murdered her son. I've tried to tell her that her son took his own life but she doesn't listen. She said if Josette hadn't done what she did, her Robbie would still be alive. She comes to see me every year on the anniversary of the day he died. I've been watching her and waiting for the opportunity to find something on this woman that I can use against her. I have a feeling this woman is bad news. The kids in her care won't talk to us or Social Services. They're too terrified, even after they left her care." He tapped the edge of the file on the table and took a step away then stopped and stared at Deke. "Can I ask why this compound is on lockdown?"

"What makes you think it is?" Deke asked.

"I know what a lockdown looks like. You have men walking inside the fence, armed to the teeth, you're setting up spotlights at key points, and you're stopping vehicles outside the main gate. All of that means something to me." Cocking his head he asked, "Are you expecting trouble?"

Deke picked up his glass and drank what was left. "Just everyday stuff I'm afraid. We just don't want anyone knowing our business."

Sullivan nodded. Reaching into his pocket, he drew out a card and laid it on the table. "Before I left Boston I heard a rumor. The way I understand it, Mrs. Pierce employed three different individuals to hunt down the girls and bring them back to Boston."

"Do these three individuals have names?" Deke asked.

"Joey Holden, Michael Winger and Jeb Carlyle. These men are lowlifes. They don't stop until they get whatever they're after and they don't care about hurting someone standing between them and what they want."

Deke glanced over to Gator who shrugged his shoulders. Turning back to Sullivan, he waited.

"I think I'll stick around town. I need some rest and I might as well get a good night's sleep before I leave for Boston." He headed toward the door. "My phone number is on the card, if you need it."

Deke watched him walk out of the clubhouse. Neither he nor Gator said a word for the longest time. Then Deke suggested, "Let's see what we can find out about the three men."

"I can give Rusty a call."

"Make sure you get pictures. I want to know what these bastards look like. If they come here looking for the girls, I want to look into their faces when they die."

Gator nodded. "What are you going to do with the girls?"

"Hell if I know." Deke scoffed. "Cassie isn't telling me anything more than I need to know and Peaches is so scared, all she can do is cry. What the hell am I supposed to do with that?"

"You think there's more to their story?" Gator asked.

"Oh, I know there is." Deke nodded. "But neither girl is willing to tell me what that is."

"Maybe you should let Sullivan take them back to Boston," Gator suggested.

Deke shook his head. "Something else happened the night they left and I want to know what it is. I think Peaches might tell us but I want Cassie to do the telling. I need her to trust me enough to tell me the truth."

"Do you think Sullivan will charge Cassie with murder?"

"I think when all the facts come out, he'll arrest this Pierce bitch for more than just murder."

Gator got to his feet. "I'll get Rusty doing his thing."

Deke got up and walked to the kitchen. He knew he needed to clear his head and the only thing that would do that was strong black coffee. He entered and Reva spun around with a knife in her hand. Deke frowned. "What the hell?"

Reva laid the knife down on the counter and took a deep breath. "Sorry Deke, you startled me. I didn't hear you come in."

"Do you know where the girls are?" he asked as he poured himself a cup of coffee.

Reva turned and looked at the far corner.

Deke followed her gaze and frowned.

Both Cassie and Peaches were sleeping, covered with a blanket.

"That girl is close to her breaking point. She can't take much more," Reva spoke quietly.

"Honey, I don't want her broken. I just want the truth to come out. She's had a hard life and no one has ever stood up for her. I want her to know I'll be there for her. That she can lean on me when she has to."

"Then stop bullying her. Let her come to you," Reva told him.

"There isn't time for that," Deke growled. "The cops just left and now, we have three very dangerous men coming our way."

"I heard."

Wiley came in just then and Deke suggested, "Let's move the girls to somewhere more comfortable." He nodded at Wiley.

Wiley looked troubled.

"What?" Deke asked.

"I-I can't touch her."

Deke cracked a smile. "I can put Cassie in my room while you put Peaches in another room."

Deke went over and gathered Cassie in his arms. He carried her to his bedroom and watched as Wiley carried Peaches down the hall to another room. Neither of them woke up. As Deke took the papers from her hand and pulled the blanket up over her shoulder, a single tear rolled down her cheek. He leaned over and kissed her forehead. Then he went over to the chair in the corner and sat down.

Having nothing better to do, he began looking over the evidence again. He hadn't really had a chance to look closely at the items Cassie kept hidden for more than half her life but he had time to search through it now.

One of the items was a small notebook. He opened the cover and began to read what was written there. At first, it didn't make sense to him and he flipped through the pages quickly. Then he went back to the beginning and started reading it again. On the third page, something clicked. Everything in the book was coded. All he had to do was figure out the code. Frustrated, he turned the next couple of pages and found something he could figure out. It was a list of initials along with monies paid.

Deke rubbed his jaw as he stared at the list of payments. He didn't know what it meant but he would bet Cassie knew. The list was several pages long and some of the payments had a plus sign in front of them. Deke figured that plus sign meant money coming in. Things were beginning to make sense now but he needed confirmation. If what he thought was going on, was really happening, it was a fucked up mess.

With a heavy sigh, he closed the book and laid his head back against the chair. Closing his eyes, he tried to clear his mind but he found he couldn't. Opening his eyes a fraction, he stared at Cassie. Had she figured out what the Pierce woman was doing? Was that her dirty little secret?

Deke rubbed his fingers across his forehead trying to relieve the pain of his headache. He paused when he heard footsteps stopping at his door. He got up and opened the door.

Gator stood there with his hand raised as if to knock.

"Did you make the call?"

Gator nodded. "I don't think you're gonna like what Rusty had to say about those three."

Deke stepped out of his room and walked a few feet down the hall. Turning to Gator, he prompted, "Tell me."

"When I gave him the names he hadn't heard of Holden or Winger but he knew the name Jeb Carlyle."

"How did he know that name?"

Gator rubbed his fingers along his jaw. "Carlyle is one tough sonofabitch. Rusty says he likes to play and he plays rough. Word around Boston is he's connected to a string of street women who have turned up almost beaten to death."

"Fuck." Deke swore.

"He said he would find out what he could about the other two and forward their photos to your phone."

Deke nodded, handing the notebook to Gator. "Take this to Zipper and have him look at it. Don't leave him alone with it. Stand over top of him and don't let that book out of your sight. I want to know what it means." Deke turned, but turned back, "Oh, and Gator, before you find Zipper, go give your woman a kiss. She deserves it."

Gator grinned and took off toward the kitchen.

Deke returned to the bedroom and found Cassie sitting on the bed going through the evidence. She looked up at him with panic in her eyes. "Where is it? It's not here! How can it not be here?"

"What are you looking for?" Deke frowned.

"The little notebook. It was here earlier."

Deke sat down next to her. Very carefully, he took her hands in his. "I gave the notebook to Gator. I have a man who might be able to decode it."

Cassie stared at his hand. Pulling hers loose from his hold, she scooted away from him. "You had no right to take it."

"Do you know what was in that book?"

Cassie nodded.

"Lance Sullivan came to see us today. He said the bitch is putting pressure on the police to find you. She wants you charged with Robbie's murder. I think you should talk to him. Tell him what really happened that night and what's been happening ever since."

"Why?" Cassie tilted her head and stared at him.

"He could stop it from happening again. You could save some other kid from living your nightmare."

"How do you know Lance Sullivan's name isn't in that book?" she asked quietly.

Deke felt his heart stop. He hadn't thought about that. "Do you know if it is?"

Cassie shook her head.

"We'll wait and see if Zipper can make heads or tails of the list of payouts I found."

"Maybe you should just let us go," Cassie suggested. "We're more trouble than we're worth."

Deke brushed a lock of hair behind her ear. "You and Peaches aren't going anywhere. We'll take care of you."

"But you don't even know us."

"You're right, I don't know you, but I do know you belong here with me and my boys," Deke whispered. "Besides, I can't let you go now. You're mine and I won't let you go."

Cassie stared at him with steady eyes.

Deke met her gaze straight on. "This club protects its own. I also think you should know the bitch sent three men after you and Peaches. For some reason, she wants you brought back to Boston. I don't think she plans to turn you over to the cops."

Cassie shivered. "She doesn't. She sold me to a man a long time ago and he's too powerful to let me go. She has to make good on the sale or face his wrath." Shrugging, she said, "I've managed to avoid it for eleven years."

"He still wants you?" Deke frowned.

"Probably not...But she does. She told me that if I didn't cooperate with the sale, she would make my life a living hell. She knows she can hurt me more by hurting Peaches. She would make me watch while she hurts my friends."

"Fucking bitch," Deke seethed.

Suddenly, the silence was shattered by the sound of gunshots echoing in the distance.

Deke ran for the door. He turned and ordered, "You stay here. Do not leave this room." Then he was gone.

CHAPTER SEVEN

Cassie heard footsteps running from every direction, then she heard nothing. A few minutes later, the door flew open as Reva and Peaches joined her.

Reva was holding a gun in her hands and she shooed them into the corner behind the bed. She closed and locked the door then joined the girls in the corner.

Then after what seemed like forever, they finally heard slow even footsteps coming down the hall toward the door. Reva held her gun a little tighter and aimed it square at the door. Moving her thumb, they heard a click as she took the safety off.

"Reva," Deke called out. "It's me, don't shoot."

Reva closed her eyes and lowered her weapon. Flipping the safety back on, she called out, "Come on in."

The door opened. Deke, Gator and Wiley came in.

Deke looked over at them. "Are you girls okay?"

Reva nodded. "We're good. Did anyone get hurt?"

"Cutter took a through and through in his arm," Gator answered. "He'll be okay. Doc is checking him out now."

Reva got to her feet and went to the main room with her husband, leaving Deke and Wiley with the other two women.

Cassie helped Peaches up from the floor and they too made their way to where the others were standing, the crowd parted and Cassie could see the man that got hurt. Blood ran down his arm.

The man everyone called Doc was cleaning his wound. He looked up and announced, "It's a clean wound. All he needs is a band-aid and a drink. It could have been worse."

"What happened out there?" Deke demanded.

Cutter glanced up. "I saw some movement in the woods outside the fence. Before I could take stock, I felt the burn of a bullet. I returned fire and some of the other boys joined me. Whoever was out there ran off. I don't know if he was hit or not."

Deke ran his fingers through his hair. "We need to stay alert, boys. Cutter saw one man but there could be as many as three trying to get in here. Get those lights on. Make it impossible for them to get in. Stay in the shadows and out of the line of fire." Deke met the gazes of his men. "We'll go on four and four. Half of you guys rest, the other half on guard duty. Change places every four hours."

Everyone went to their places. Some of the guys went outside while the rest headed to the rooms down the hall beyond Deke's bedroom.

Deke walked over to one of his guys sitting in the corner. He was at a small table, scribbling on a piece of paper. "Zipper, have you had any luck?"

Zipper looked up and nodded. "You were right, it's a log of payments coming in and going out. There are no names listed, only initials but anyone who knows anybody in Boston, might be able to tell you who these people are." He leaned back in his chair. "This book covers an eight year time span. It has twelve sales listed."

Deke nodded. "That book is at least eleven years old. Since then, she's probably sold dozens more."

"What exactly is she selling?" Zipper asked.

"Do you really want to know?"

Zipper nodded and waited for Deke to answer.

"She's selling kids," Deke told him. "Very young kids."

Zipper stared at him, then shook his head. "I know we don't work with the badges but we need to do everything we can to stop this bitch, cuz that's just wrong. Any way you fucking slice it, selling kids is wrong."

Deke motioned his head to the notebook. "Is the name Lance Sullivan listed in there under outgoing payments?"

Zipper shook his head. "Not that I found."

"Then let's hope he's an honest badge. Maybe we can give this information to him and he can bust her ass."

~* * * *~

A short time later, Cassie looked around the room for Peaches and found her on the sofa sleeping. Some of the men were sitting at the other tables talking quietly. She could see Deke and Gator at one of the other tables. She got to her feet and joined Reva in the kitchen.

She didn't say anything. She just went to the corner and slid down the wall. Pulling her knees up to her chest, she rested her chin on them. For a long time, neither of them spoke.

Finally, Cassie asked the question, "Why is Deke doing this for me? I'm nobody. Why is he risking his life and everyone else's for a woman he doesn't even know? I don't understand."

Reva cut through the sandwich she was making, then laid the knife down. Without turning her head, she replied, "Some people look at these guys like they're shit they just stepped in. Not many people understand who or what these guys are. All they can see is that they're bikers. Big bad asses that belong to a club." Picking up her knife again, she continued, "And they are all of that, but so much more. Belonging to a MC club doesn't mean these guys don't care. We're a family. Hell, most of these guys joined the club just to belong somewhere. Some of them are misfits, some of them just like to be bad, but like everybody else, they're human."

Cassie listened and thought about the warmth she saw in Deke's eyes and what she thought about him the first time she saw him. He wasn't like what she thought at first.

"Being in a club isn't easy for everyone and not everyone can live this life, but it's a damn good life for those who can. We all work for a common goal and we all stand together to protect this way of life. We love together and the guys protect what they have. They can be a rowdy bunch but you'll never find a better group of men." She hesitated briefly then added, "I don't know what these guys do for a living, other than the dance club but that's not my business. That's club business and we know enough not to ask. That's one of the rules we all live by."

Her explanation blew Cassie away. She thought clubs like this one lived dangerously, looking to break the law rather than uphold it. "Is that true for all clubs?"

Reva shook her head. "No baby girl, I've seen other clubs and not all of them are like this one. This is one of the better ones."

Cassie laid her head down on her knees. "I've never really belonged to anything good before. Me and Peaches had to make our own way for a long time. We were all we had." She sighed. "It must be nice to belong to someone and something like this."

Reva smiled. "It is...it's very nice."

"Is Deke one of the good guys?" Cassie whispered.

"Yes, he is, Oh, don't get me wrong, he can be a badass when he wants to be. He's a hard man, but he's fair. I think he'd be good for you."

Cassie closed her eyes. "I'm so tired of running, always looking over my shoulder, never knowing when trouble is going to find us. There have been a few times when I just wanted to give up. Go somewhere and just curl up and quit. I would have too, if not for Peaches. She needed me. I had to stay strong for her."

~****~

When she didn't hear anything for a few minutes, Reva looked over and found Cassie was asleep again. There were shadows under her eyes and her skin almost appeared bruised. Her eyebrows looked tight as if her dreams upset her.

Shaking her head, Reva had to wonder what demons held this child in their grasp. She figured it was bad. Gator came in to refill his coffee cup. She met his eyes and jerked her head to where Cassie was sleeping.

Gator followed her eyes and when he saw her, his fingers curled tighter around his cup.

Reva came closer to her husband and whispered in his ear, "She's been all the way to hell and back hasn't she?"

Gator wrapped his big arms around his woman. "Yup, she has."

Reva met his eyes. "Bad?"

"Worse than you can imagine."

"Can you guys save her?" Reva asked.

"We have to…Deke won't let her go and heaven help anyone who tries to take her away from him." He glanced over at the girl. "Do you think we should move her?"

Reva shook her head. "Let her sleep. At least for now, the demons are leaving her alone."

Gator kissed his woman, then poured his coffee and went back to the main room.

Reva poured herself a cup and joined him. Things were slow right now and she prayed they would stay that way.

~****~

Cassie slept undisturbed for the next few hours. When she came awake again, her mind was clear and she felt a calm she hadn't felt in some time. She stretched her arms over her head and slowly got to her feet. Her body felt recharged and she was filled with an energy she knew she would have to explore.

Peeking out into the main room, she could see everyone was quiet, most everyone seemed to be resting. Deke was in a chair leaning against the wall, his eyes closed in slumber. Gator was lying on a mattress someone had hauled into the room and he was holding Reva in his arms. They too, had their eyes closed.

Peaches was curled up on the couch. Behind her was Wiley and his arms held her. Cassie could see other mattresses along the wall. Men were laying on them and she could hear snoring echoing in the quiet.

She suddenly had the overwhelming urge to paint. So much so, that she could picture exactly what she wanted to draw. She went to the back room and began looking at the cans of paint she'd discovered the other day.

Gathering what she would need, she carried it out to the main room. The only spot that was open was next to her painting of Rufus. It was a huge area next to the back door. Opening the black paint, she dipped her brush and began to paint. Her lines were bold and everything just came together quickly. So lost in her art, she barely heard the door open nor care as the men changed places.

Some laid down to sleep but there were one or two that laid there and watched her work.

Deke opened his eyes and in the silence, he watched her painting come to life.

The scent of paint brought Gator and Reva back to the land of the living. They too, didn't move but watched as Cassie worked.

As the sun came up, Peaches opened her eyes and gasped softly. Wiley began to move behind her and she reached behind her to cover his mouth with her hand.

Wiley's eyes widened as he caught sight of what everyone else could see.

A single beam of light shone on the painting and when Cassie put her brush down—that beam of light seemed to bring her painting to life. As she stood there oblivious to the room around her, she felt arms surrounding her from behind. Her heart began pounding in her chest and she felt a moment of fear. For the span of a heartbeat, she felt her fight or flight response kick in, then she recognized a familiar scent and relaxed. She knew he would never hurt her.

"He's beautiful," Deke whispered in her ear. He stared at her painting. The huge cat's face almost appeared real. He could see the gleam in the lion's eyes, as if he had just caught sight of his next meal. The cat's mouth was set in a snarl and Deke could see a dribble of saliva gleaming off the teeth.

"I call him Diablo," Cassie spoke quietly. She was tired now. Bringing her painting to life had drained her earlier burst of energy.

"He's beautiful Cass," Peaches told her friend.

Cassie turned her head and smiled. "I always did like the big cats."

Peaches smiled gently. "Yeah, you always did." She stared at the painting again. "I feel as if he's seconds away from ripping into my body with those teeth."

The doors opened and several men came in to break the silence of the room. When they saw the new painting, they stopped and stared.

Reva got up from her place on the floor and as she passed Cassie and Deke, she reached out and patted Cassie on the arm.

Cassie bent over and began cleaning up her paint cans. Carrying them to the kitchen, she ran water through the brushes. The aroma of freshly brewed coffee hit her. When she shook out the water from the brushes, she felt Peaches come up behind her. Cassie turned to look at her.

Peaches was smiling at her. "He is so beautiful."

"Thanks." Cassie nodded.

"You're in a good place, aren't you?" her friend whispered.

"It doesn't make sense does it?" Cassie pondered.

"For whatever it's worth, I think Deke is good for you."

Cassie paused, then said, "His touch excites the hell out of me."

Peaches cocked her head and asked, "And that bothers you? That would be a good thing, don't you think?"

"It could be if I didn't feel he was holding back," Cassie admitted.

"Holding back?" Peaches frowned.

"Every time we get together, he's wonderful but I feel like he's holding the best part from me. He makes me feel things I never thought I would and my body responds to his touch but there is a hint of something bigger and better in his eyes. I don't know what it is and he has me curious."

"That could be a good thing too." Peaches grinned.

"Can I say something?" Reva broke in.

Cassie and Peaches turned to gaze at her.

"You've made it very clear to everyone here you can't stand to be touched. Deke respects that. He knows some of what you've been through and he doesn't want to hurt you. But honey, there's a good touch and a bad touch. Sharing your body with someone you care about is a good thing. I know some women who only want a gentle touch and they look for men to give it to them. These men aren't gentle lovers. They prefer their loving hot and heavy. Now, I've had gentle loving and I've had it hot and heavy. But if you ask me, I like it so much more when it's hot and heavy. I love the feeling Gator gives me when he shares my body but when he gets down and dirty, it's so much better for both of us."

"Does Deke like it down and dirty, do you think?" Cassie asked.

Reva snorted. "Deke and Gator are the same kind of men. They both like to live on the edge. They like to work hard and play hard. Big and bad and they like to bend the rules to suit themselves. I think they like loving the same way."

"So, you think he's holding back?"

"He might be afraid of breaking you," Reva admitted. "Deke has never been an easy man but with you, I see something I've never seen before. He actually cares about you. Believe me when I tell you, I don't think the man has ever cared for a woman before. They were here for his pleasure but he never thought about their feelings before."

"So you know him better than I do," Cassie said. "How do I get him to show me real loving? I've never known that before and before something happens, I want to feel everything I can. I might have to live on those memories for a long time when I leave here."

Reva patted her hands. "All you have to do is ask him. Let him know what you want, then you hold on and let yourself be unafraid. He isn't going to hurt you."

Cassie nodded. Then she had to ask, "What's going on out there? Why have men been coming and going at all hours?"

"It's club business and you should ask Deke about that."

"Do you know?"

Reva hesitated then nodded.

"Can you tell me?"

"I really shouldn't stick my neck out. It's Deke's business."

"Can you tell me if it has to do with me and Peaches?" Cassie begged.

"Yeah, honey, it does," Reva finally told her.

"Are we putting these men in danger?"

Reva sighed heavily. "Honey, they are protecting you from some very bad men looking for you. That's all I know." She turned away.

"Reva, "Cassie called out. When the other woman turned back she asked, "Has anyone else come looking for us?"

Reva nodded. "Some cop came yesterday.

Cassie turned to Peaches and sweat formed on her brow. She reached her hand out and Peaches grabbed it.

~* * * *~

Deke was staring at the new painting.

Suddenly, Wiley came in. "Hey boss."

Deke turned and glanced at him. "What's up?"

"We have a visitor."

"Oh, and who might that be?" Deke asked.

"A Boston badge. You want we should let him parlay?"

Deke thought for a moment, then looked toward the kitchen. "Hang on a minute and I'll let you know." He headed to the room he knew Cassie and Peaches were in.

When he came through the door, Cassie and Peaches turned to stare at him. They had a slightly panicked look in their eyes.

"Lance Sullivan is here. He's a Boston badge and he's been looking for you two for a long time now." He paused for a moment and asked, "Do you want to see him?"

Cassie turned to Peaches. "Are you ready for this?"

"Not really..." Peaches whispered.

"It has to happen at some point," Cassie reminded her friend.

Deke took a few steps closer. "You and Peaches aren't alone in this. I'm here to protect you as well as every other man here. You belong to us now and we don't give up or let go of what belongs to us."

Cassie took a deep breath and exhaled. Her fingers tightened on Peaches' grip. "You won't let him take us back to Boston?"

Deke wrapped his hand around the back of Cassie's neck and pulled her closer. When their lips were almost touching he whispered, "You aren't going anywhere, but I do think you should tell this badge your story. I think you guys have run long enough, now it's time to turn and make your stand."

"Do you think he'll listen to what we have to say?" Peaches asked.

Deke turned his head to view her. "I think he wants to."

Cassie touched her forehead to his briefly. "Let's do this before I lose my nerve."

Deke reached down and twined his fingers with hers. He slowly tugged both girls to the door and into the main room.

Wiley watched him carefully. At Deke's nod, he walked out the door.

Moments later, Wiley ushered Detective Sullivan into the room.

Deke had taken a seat at one of the tables along with Cassie and Peaches. Five of the other bikers, including Gator, stood behind Deke and the girls.

Sullivan paused when he saw all of them, then continued to the table. He met Deke's eyes then his curious gaze moved on to Cassie and Peaches. "I had to come back today." He raised his gaze to the painting on the wall. His eyes widened when he saw the new painting next to the tiger. His mouth dropped open as he took in the bold lines and swirl of colors. He turned to stare at Cassie. Then, he transferred his gaze to Deke.

With a wave of his hand, Deke invited him to sit

When Sullivan sat down, he searched the girl's faces. "I came here to find Josette Rearden and Callie Blake. I wanted to ask them about their story. I'm not here to hurt you and if I don't like what I hear. I'll do whatever I have to do to see that you girls are safe. You have my word on that."

"You'll forgive me Detective, if I don't trust you altogether." Cassie sneered. "The people who should have protected us, were either were blind to what was going on right under their noses or they were too busy stuffing their pockets with payoff money to give a shit about the welfare of the unwanted kids in your foster system."

"Can you tell me?" Sullivan asked.

"Are you sure you want to hear the details?"

Sullivan sighed and nodded. "When this case hit my desk eleven years ago, the file read assault with pending charges of attempted murder. Robbie Pierce's medical records were part of that file and what happened to him was bad, really bad.' He paused and stared at Cassie. "When I first read the age of the perpetrator I had to stop and read it several times. It listed your age as being ten years old. Is that right?"

Cassie nodded slowly. "I was only ten at the time, yes."

"Then I asked myself why or what would make a ten year old little girl do such a thing? I couldn't wrap my mind around it, so I began asking questions. Nobody had any answers, at least none that I could live with, so I began digging deeper. The deeper I dug, the less I could come up with. My Captain told me to leave it alone. He told me no good could come of it. He said Mrs. Pierce had a lot of high profile friends and he asked me if I thought this inquiry was worth my job."

"In other words, he was on her payroll." Deke sneered.

Sullivan shook his head. "I can't believe that. Captain Rainer is a good man." He turned back to Cassie, "Tell me what happened."

Reva came in and set a cup of coffee in front of her.

Cassie wrapped her cold fingers around the cup and began her story. She told them about the years of torture and pain within the Pierce household.

As she told her story, one by one most of the members of the club came in and stood quietly behind the table.

She told about her father bringing his three year old daughter to Eleonore's home. She told them how much money Eleonore gave him and how he walked away without looking back to even say goodbye. Everyone listened to the heartbreak she had gone through.

Peaches had tears running down her face as Cassie searched her memories and told them about the first few years she had. When Cassie got to the part where Peaches came there, she turned and smiled through her tears. "When Peaches came, I finally had a friend. I couldn't let anyone hurt her, so I became her protector."

Peaches reached out and took her hand. "No one has ever given me more than you have." She looked around at everyone standing there listening. "When things got really bad, Cassie would always be there for me and the other kids. She would sing us to sleep and hide us when she needed to. She would stand up for us and go out of her way to piss off Mrs. Pierce in order to take her attention away from the little things other kids would get in trouble for. For some reason, Mrs. Pierce enjoyed beating Cassie but her favorite punishment was tying Cassie's hands together and pushing her down into the basement. It was dark and damp and she'd be alone in the dark for days sometimes...." She paused as she sniffled through her tears. "She would take Robbie down there with her and they would hurt Cassie together. The last time she beat Cassie and threw her down there, she sent Robbie down by himself. Then we heard Cassie screaming. When she stopped, Robbie came upstairs and told his mother he taught her a good lesson."

Sullivan turned his head and studied Cassie's face. It was closed off. He could see a tick in her jaw as she clenched her teeth. "What happened in the basement Cassie? What did he do to you?"

Cassie wouldn't answer him. No one had ever known what happened that day except for Peaches and she didn't want to tell them.

Sullivan waited for her answer and when it didn't come, he turned to Peaches. "When did this happen?"

"Two days before we left," Peaches whispered.

"Do you know what he did to her?" Sullivan asked.

Peaches nodded but didn't say anything. Fresh tears ran down her cheeks.

Finally, Deke growled, "Tell this man what the little bastard did to her."

"No!" Cassie shouted as she jumped to her feet. Her face was pale and she was crying. "It's my secret to tell or keep and I will not share it with anyone."

Peaches got up and went to stand in front of Cassie. Putting her hands around Cassie's face she whispered, "Please tell them. They want to understand why you hurt Robbie. It's time to let go of your secret." She leaned forward until her forehead touched Cassie's. "You've protected that little bastard for too long. It's time the truth was finally told. Please..."

Cassie wrapped her arms around Peaches. Turning her head, she stared at Sullivan. "After Mrs. Pierce beat the living hell out of me, she tied my hands together and dragged me downstairs again. When she tied the rope to the wall, I thought she'd leave me alone in the dark again. I was in so much pain from the beating I didn't care. I thought about giving up and letting the darkness take me but I knew Peaches still needed me. Then Robbie came downstairs. He had a nasty look on his face. I could see it because the lights were still on. He came closer to me and began taking his clothes off. My mind went blank and I don't really know what happened. When I came back from wherever

I'd gone he was cutting me. The little bastard liked to cut people. The pain was unbearable and I couldn't contain it. I screamed and didn't finish until he was done. When he finally wiped the knife clean he told me everyone would know who and what I was from then on."

"What did he mean by that?" Sullivan asked.

"He left scars on my body, just like his mother did that day," Cassie said. Her words were whispered but everyone in the room heard them.

Deke frowned. He hadn't noticed the scar she spoke about.

Peaches leaned forward and spoke softly, "You have to show them."

Cassie backed away while shaking her head.

Peaches stopped her as she said, "If you want the truth to come out, you have to show them what he did to you, what he planned to do to me the night we left."

Cassie closed her eyes and knew she didn't have a choice. She turned around and ripped the buttons of her shirt open. As she lowered the shirt from her shoulders, everyone in the room could see her skin. Exposed there on her back was her worst shame. She wasn't wearing a bra and her whole back was exposed to their gazes.

She heard gasps and could imagine what these people were thinking. Most of her back was scarred by the belt she'd been beaten with. The worst of the scars had faded but were still there and would be until she died. The evidence of what Robbie had done to her was on her upper back along her shoulder blades. The letters were carved deep and had taken a long time to heal.

WHORE was the word Robbie Pierce had carved into her back.

Cassie broke down and ran down the back hall. She tried to pull her shirt back up to cover her shame. The door to Deke's bedroom slammed and they all heard her sobs.

~ * * * * ~

Deke's fingers crushed the shot glass in his hand until it shattered. The glass cut deep and his blood mixed with the liquor inside of it. In all the time he'd been with her, he had never taken the time to really see her. He never knew about the scars she carried. He hadn't cared enough to look. No wonder she would curl up in a blanket.

Peaches sat down at the table but couldn't look at anyone. "Robbie cornered me that day," she continued the story Cassie had started. "There was no one else home. He thought Cassie was still tied up in the basement and he dragged me to the playroom. He ripped my clothes off and tied me up. Then he was getting his knife ready. He kept bragging that I would have the same brand as Cassie." She swallowed hard. "I began to scream and Robbie was laughing at me. He told me I could make as much noise as I wanted. There was no one who cared, and no one who would stop him." She shook her head. "He was wrong. Cassie was there. When I started screaming, she had broken through the ropes and came looking for me. I could see the blood on her wrists and at first, she couldn't even hold the knife. Her fingers couldn't wrap around the handle and she kept trying to grip it. Then she saw the look of terror on my face and she came after Robbie. I've never seen her s-so angry..." Peaches halted as she looked away and seemed to be reliving it.

The people in the room were silent and some looked pale while others looked enraged.

"When Robbie saw her, he backed away from me but she was having a hard time holding on to the knife. He thought she couldn't hurt him but he was wrong. She cut him good. Rage had given her the strength to do what she thought had to be done. By the time she was finished, he was the one screaming. After she dropped the knife, she untied my hands and got both of us the hell out of there. She made a stop to get some food and bottled water, then she went to get the evidence she'd been collecting the past few months and went into the den. All of us kids knew we weren't allowed in the den. Mrs. Pierce ordered us never to go into that room, but Cassie went in there and when she came back out, she had the book and some money."

"What book?' Sullivan asked.

"Part of her evidence was a small notebook that listed Mrs. Pierce's activities," Deke explained. "Money from sales and money paid out to the people in her network."

"Sales? What was she selling?" Sullivan looked perplexed.

Deke stared at the man. "She was selling the babies in her care."

Sullivan paled. "Does she still have the book?" he whispered.

Zipper broke away from his spot and grabbed everything he'd been searching through earlier. He dumped it on the table in front of Sullivan. With a disgusted grunt, he went back to where he'd been standing earlier.

"You can look at that shit but you ain't taking it out of here unless Cassie gives you her permission," Deke told him. "She's trusting you with her life. Hers and Peaches and if you fuck her over, we will return the favor. Each man jack of us will hunt you down and take a piece of you."

Sullivan raised his head up and stared at Deke. "Don't worry, I won't let them down. This Pierce woman may have friends but she doesn't have you guys on her side. I think hell is coming for Mrs. Pierce."

Deke nodded. "Do you remember those men you told us might be coming here after the girls?"

Sullivan continued to stare at him.

"One of them showed up last night. He shot one of my men and they shot back. We don't know if he was hit or not, but those bastards are not getting to Cassie or Peaches. They belong to us now, and we will keep them safe."

Sullivan shrugged. "Then you do whatever you have to do. I'll let the local LEOS know what's going on, so if they end up dead they won't come after you guys."

Deke let out a cold laugh. "Yeah, you do that. If those guys show up and we kill them, their bodies will never be found. On that you have my word."

Sullivan glanced back at Peaches and asked her, "How did the two of you escape?"

Peaches shrugged. "There was no one else home that night, but Cassie wouldn't take the chance anyone would stop us, so we went through the woods behind the house. The kids were afraid of those woods, so we never went there. Mrs. Pierce always told us there were dangerous people living in the woods and if we went there, they would get us. She said they would hurt us and finally kill us. But the truth was, she was the evil that would kill us."

"Where did you go after you got away?" Sullivan asked.

"Cassie was in pretty bad shape. She hadn't had the time she needed to completely heal from the beating and what Robbie did to her. She knew we needed to get away and she went as far as she could. We found a cave near the water and I made her stop. I cleaned her up the best I could and we stayed there for three days. I wanted her to stay longer but we ran out of food and water. We traveled at night because she didn't want to be seen."

"Where did you go after that?" Sullivan questioned.

"We stayed in Boston for a couple of years," Peaches replied. "Living in the shadows, we learned to survive. Then one night Cassie was attacked. They hurt her bad before she got away from them. Two days after that, the bastards that hurt her came looking to finish the job, so she knew we couldn't stay there anymore. We left Boston and followed the ocean south. We were in Rhode Island for a while, then went to Connecticut then we went back to Massachusetts for a while then we came here to New York."

"How did you live?"

"We had some money in the beginning, but that only lasted a couple of years. Cassie got very good at stealing what she needed until we looked old enough to work. She would get jobs at fast food places. One thing she insisted on was for both of us to finish school. We both took online classes. We knew we couldn't go to school, so we would visit the library every day and use their computers and we both passed the GED test when we were sixteen."

Before anyone could say a word, they all heard a scream.

Deke and the others ran toward the bedroom where Cassie was.

Sullivan stood up as well but Wiley prevented him from following the others. "Why don't you just sit here and wait?" Wiley suggested to him.

CHAPTER EIGHT

Cassie slammed the door behind her. Picking up a shirt off the floor, she pulled it over her shoulders. The shirt she wore earlier wouldn't close as she had ripped off the buttons. Tears streamed down her face and she stumbled toward the bed where she grabbed the blanket off and wrapped it around her shoulders. Walking over to the corner, she slid down the wall and brought her knees up. Wrapping the blanket around her, she laid her head on her knees and let shame and guilt wash over her.

Shame because of the word cut into her skin and guilt because of what she'd done to Robbie. She knew she shouldn't feel either sensation but she could still remember her mother's soft words. *Do onto others as you would have do unto you.* She could no longer see her sweet face but she did remember the sound of her voice. It never made sense since she had done to Robbie what he'd done to her, really.

Suddenly, she was pulled from her misery as someone grabbed her hair. For a moment, she couldn't believe someone could just show up here in the room. Before he hauled her to her feet, her hands wrapped around something heavy. With the blanket hiding her body from him, she kept her hand hidden.

"Well, well, well. What do we have here?" The stranger asked. "Are you one of the bitches we came here to find?" Cassie struggled but he just tightened his grip until he had her on her tiptoes. "Now, now, none of that. Which bitch are you, Cassie or Peaches?" Then he shrugged. "You better be worth all this."

"Who are you?" Cassie gasped. "How did you get in here?"

"Never mind that now." He pulled on her hair again. "Ellie wants me to carry your sorry ass back to Boston...she's willing to pay big bucks to get you back."

Cassie sneered at him. "You're one of her flunkies?"

The man grabbed her chin. His fingers bit into her skin and he wasn't bothered when she hissed in pain. "I ain't nobody's flunky, bitch."

Cassie narrowed her eyes. "Don't touch me."

The man laughed at her. "Hell, I'll do more than touch you bitch. Ellie said to bring you back to her alive, but she didn't say anything about bruised and beaten."

Just then, another man stuck his head in the window. "Come on Jeb, hustle it up. They're bound to make another trip around the fence line soon."

Jeb turned to glare at the man. "Get the fuck away from the window. Get back to cover. I'll be right out with this bitch."

As soon as the other man disappeared from sight, she raised the wrench. "I fucking don't like people touching me!" She screamed as the wrench hit his skull.

Jeb dropped to one knee. Blood ran down the side of his face and when he looked up, he snarled. "I'm gonna enjoy beating the hell out of you, bitch!"

Cassie threw the blanket off her shoulders. Backing away a step or two, she held the wrench up with one hand and motioned for him to come after her. "Come on you bastard, come get me."

Jeb rushed her and Cassie sidestepped him. She brought the wrench down on his back.

He fell onto the bed. He got back up and came at her again. He grabbed her by the arm and brought her close to him.

Cassie could feel the heat from his body and smell the stink of his breath. She shuddered in revulsion and stomped her foot down on his, when he grunted but didn't move away, she brought her knee up then slammed him in the groin.

Jeb bent over in pain but still held her by the arm.

Cassie growled, "Let me go, you bastard." Raising her hand up, she hit him in the head again with the wrench.

Jeb grunted and slid to the floor.

She raised her foot and kicked him several times in the ribs and back, but Jeb didn't feel them. He laid there unconscious and bleeding.

Cassie raised her foot again to kick him when she heard pounding on the door. Her rage began to fade when she heard Deke calling her name. Dropping the wrench, she hobbled over to the door and slid the lock open. Throwing the door open, she fell into his arms.

Deke's arms wrapped around her as he viewed his bedroom beyond her. He saw signs of a struggle complete with blood pooling around the man laid out of the floor. The window was open and there was a smear of blood on the bed. He could see the bloody wrench on the floor beside the man.

Cassie wrapped her arms around Deke. She was babbling as she pushed her face into his chest. "I told him not to touch me. I told him. I told him."

Deke leaned back so he could see her. "Are you okay baby? Did he hurt you?"

Cassie shook her head. "I told him not to touch me." She kept repeating.

Deke turned with her in his arms. He saw Gator standing behind him. "Clean this mess up, get him the hell out of here."

Cassie lifted her head. "There is another guy outside. He poked his head in the window and told this guy they had to leave."

Zipper and several others took off for the main door.

Deke half carried Cassie out to his table. When she sat down, he knelt beside her and asked, "What the hell happened in here?"

Cassie shook her head. "I was sitting in the corner with my head down. I didn't see him at all then he grabbed me by my hair and yanked me up. I didn't even realize I had the wrench in my hand until I hit him with it."

"Did he say anything?"

"Only that Mrs. Pierce promised to pay him to return us to Boston."

Deke looked enraged. "What happened then?"

"He got mad at me when I called him a flunky. He grabbed my chin and I told him not to touch me again. He said he was going to enjoy hurting me and I kinda lost it." Cassie shook her head. "I told him but he wouldn't listen."

Deke smiled and he had to chuckle. "Yeah...I'll bet he wishes he would've listened." He stood and walked her out to the main room.

They watched as Gator dragged Jeb's body through the main room and out the door. Deke looked over at Sullivan. "Are we going to have a problem here?"

Sullivan shrugged. "I didn't see anything."

Deke gave him a nod, then glanced back at Cassie. "Are you gonna be okay if I leave for a little bit? I have some business to take care of."

Cassie looked over at Peaches and nodded. "We'll be fine."

Deke got to his feet and turned to Wiley. "Watch over them." When Wiley nodded, Deke turned to follow his men out the door.

~****~

Deke strode over to where his men were standing in a circle. Pushing his way through their line, he viewed the two men inside the manmade circle.

Jeb was just coming to.

However, the other man was on his knees and sobbing. Someone had given him several deep bruises on his face and neck. He was ranting, "I had nothing to do with what happened. I never hurt the girl!"

"But you came here thinking you were gonna snatch her away from us, didn't you?" Deke growled. "You would have hurt her, given the chance."

The man shook his head. "We were supposed to grab the girls and take them back to Boston, that's all. That crazy dame wanted them alive. I have no idea what Jeb or Michael were going to do with them."

Deke looked at Gator, then dropped his gaze to the man on the ground. "Your name is Joey, right?"

Joey nodded his head.

Now Deke asked, "Where is Michael?"

Joey turned his head and stared at the woods beyond the gate. "We had to leave him in the woods. Jeb won't go back and carry him out. Mike shot at one of your guys last night and got hit by return fire. He got it good and he couldn't meet up with us. I don't know if he's even alive anymore. He wasn't looking so good the last time I saw him."

"So, Jeb's the type of man who'd leave a man behind, huh?" Deke scoffed. "What a nice guy."

Joey shook his head. "He's not a nice guy," he stated with a shudder.

"Shut the fuck up, moron." Jeb growled. Raising a hand to his head, he groaned. "What the fuck did that bitch hit me with anyway?" He didn't bother looking around as he sat up. When he finally did raise his eyes, he caught Deke's cold gaze and gave him the finger.

Deke grabbed his hair and hauled him to his feet. "How does this feel, asshole?" Deke felt blood running down his wrist as he shook Jeb.

"Fuck you, bastard!" Jeb tried to spit in his face.

Deke slammed his fist onto Jeb's jaw.

Jeb groaned as Deke allowed him to fall to the dirt. He turned back to Joey to ask, "What were you guys promised to grab the girls and take them back?"

"Mrs. Pierce promised us a hundred thousand dollars, but I think she promised Jeb something in addition to the money."

"What makes you think that?" Deke wanted to know.

"As we were leaving, she took a ring off her finger and put it in his pocket," Joey admitted. "Then she told him to have fun."

Deke sneered at him. "Why are you giving up this info on your friends?"

Joey spit on Jeb. "These guys aren't my friends. I wanted nothing to do with this. I didn't like it when Mrs. Pierce explained what the mission was and I hated having to deal with him." he kicked out at Jeb. "I don't know the girls' story but I hated that bitchy Pierce woman."

"But you still came after her," Deke stated.

"And now I'm gonna die for my stupidity?" Joey growled. "Will you tell her I'm sorry?"

Deke knelt beside the man. "What are you sorry for?"

"I overheard Jeb talking to Mike the first night we were on the road. He told him a little about the girl. If she had to endure all that shit, she didn't deserve to have to go back."

Deke got to his feet. Glaring at Gator he said, "Keep them alive and feed them to the sows."

Gator nodded as he grabbed Joey and a couple of the others grabbed Jeb. They dragged them away.

Joey had stopped whining and walked to his fate like a man.

"Find Mike's body and take him with you," Deke called out.

Gator nodded and kept on going.

"Wait a minute," Deke called out. He walked up to Jeb and searched his pockets. He fished the ring out of his front left pocket. It was gold and had a large diamond setting. With a sneer on his lips, he put the ring in his own pocket. He walked slowly back inside. He was tired. Tired of the bitch who threatened his woman and tired of the bullshit that came with her. If he could, he would ride to Boston and break her damned neck.

When he got back to the table, Cassie wouldn't look at him and Peaches looked like she was going to cry. Lance Sullivan seemed uncomfortable and Wiley looked pissed.

"What the fuck is going on here?" Deke demanded.

"The badge wants the girls to go back to Boston with him. Says he can protect them," Wiley explained while looking troubled by the suggestion.

Deke shook his head. "That ain't gonna happen, not in this lifetime."

"They will be in no danger," Sullivan insisted. "I can protect them from Mrs. Pierce."

"You don't know that for certain that you can and I'm not willing to risk their lives." Deke stabbed his finger in Sullivan's chest. "We can keep them safe here. You go back to Boston and end that bitch or I will."

Sullivan nodded. "With this stuff, I can go a long way but we need some of it decoded before we can go forward."

"Then decode this shit and get on it!" Deke shouted. "But until this is done and that bitch is either in jail or dead, the girls stay here. They are under our protection and will remain so."

"But I can't be in two places at once." Sullivan stood from his chair. "I need to be wherever they are."

"Why?" Deke questioned. "Don't you think we can protect them?"

Sullivan seemed to slump where he stood. "You don't understand. I've been working on this case for eleven years. I told myself that if I ever did find the girls, I wouldn't leave them until the case was finished. They became so much a part of my life that I have to see this through."

"But you didn't even know us," Cassie told him.

"Maybe not, but I got to know you a little, by working the case." Sullivan shrugged.

"You have no idea what we went through!" Peaches cried. "You have no idea what went on behind the walls of that house."

Sullivan snorted. "I can't say that. There have been rumors for a long time about the Pierce household."

"What kind of rumors?" Cassie asked as her face paled.

"Shortly after Robbie killed himself, Walter Pierce began drinking. He did a lot of drinking at a local bar. He told some pretty wild stories to the friends he made there. One of these friends, Jeff White, came to the police with these tales. He didn't know if he could believe them or not but he claims he wanted someone to know what was going on." Sullivan stared at Cassie briefly. "We began our investigation two years ago."

"And how close are you to nailing this bitch?" Deke demanded.

Sullivan looked down at the evidence in front of him. "This should be everything we need."

"Then get on it and get it done." Deke barked.

"I need to go back to Boston to finish this, but there's a problem." Sullivan ran his fingers through his hair. "I'm not sure who I can trust in Boston. I was looking through the book earlier and I know who some of those initials belong too."

"You know what those sales mean?" Deke asked.

Sullivan nodded. "Yeah and that's another reason we want her. She's involved in a kiddie porn ring that goes nationwide." He shrugged. "The FBI have been sniffing around. Apparently, Boston is a pick up and drop off point. We just didn't know who or where they were operating from. This ties in with what the FBI thought."

Deke looked disgusted. "How did she sell those kids without anyone knowing it? Why did no one not notice them being gone?"

Cassie snapped her head around to Deke. "Because nobody gave a shit!" she yelled. "We were all throw away kids, nobody wanted us, and there was no one to care."

"That's not true." Sullivan shook his head. "Someone cared."

Cassie got to her feet. "Do you know how I came to be in her house?"

Sullivan shook his head.

"My mother died when I was three years old," Cassie explained. "My father was a drunk and a junkie. He couldn't handle a small kid, even his own daughter. When things got bad, he took me to her house and she gave him money to keep me. Social Services didn't even know I was there. Every visit they made, she kept me hidden. There was never a file on me because they didn't know I existed. So if that's the case, how did you know my name?"

Deke frowned and looked over at Sullivan. Reaching behind his back, his fingers wrapped around the butt of his weapon. When he brought it out in front of him, he pointed it at Sullivan. "How about you answer her question? How did you know her name if no one else was aware she was there?"

Sullivan slowly raised his hands. "When Eleonore Pierce's son Robbie died she came in and began shouting about Josette Rearden and Callie Blake. Now, we had a file on Callie but we had nothing on Josette. She brought us a file on Josette. Claimed the girl was in her care for a friend. She told us the girl had only been in her care for a couple of months. The file told us the girl was troubled with a violent history. The file held some reports from another county. We had nothing else to go on."

"So, this bitch hands you a phony file and you fell for it? What does that make you, besides fucking stupid?" Deke scoffed.

"Not so stupid." Sullivan shook his head. "I realized something was wrong with the file and I did a background on the info. Josette Rearden didn't exist. The file was fake. That made me wonder why she would go to that much trouble. We did a background check on the Rearden name and found her father. Then we found her mother's grave and asked the old man some questions. We sobered him up first but he claimed his daughter was living with a friend and he couldn't care for her."

"So, the bastard didn't tell you he sold me to Mrs. Pierce?" Cassie asked.

Sullivan shook his head. "Your father was so messed up, he didn't remember where you were. He didn't know the name Eleonore Pierce at all."

Cassie shook her head. "He was always high or drunk. He blamed me and Mom for his own failures. Even when I was three, I knew that much. I remember the fights they had. I'd wake up to their screaming at each other. I doubt the man could remember his own name at times."

"That doesn't explain the sales," Deke reminded them. "How do so many kids disappear without someone noticing?"

"They didn't," Peaches whispered. "That was the big secret in that house. When she sold one of the kids, she would then replace them with another throw away kid."

"What?" Sullivan sat down with a thud and stared at her.

Cassie nodded. "You found Josette Rearden but you won't find Callie Blake."

Everyone turned to look at Peaches.

"Aren't you Callie?" Deke finally asked.

Peaches shook her head.

Cassie held out her hand to Peaches. Their fingers entwined. "No, she came after Callie disappeared," Cassie explained. "She was five years old but she'd been through a trauma and couldn't remember who she was. She couldn't even speak when she first got there. It took months before she spoke."

"Did you ever remember your name or anything about what happened to you?" Sullivan asked.

"No, I didn't," Peaches answered. She looked over at Cassie. "But that never made a difference to Cassie. She didn't care who I was or what happened to me before I came to the Pierce house."

"So, we still don't know where Callie is," Sullivan stated.

"Oh, I know where she is," Cassie admitted.

"You do?" Sullivan stared at her as he frowned.

"Yep."

"Where is she?" he demanded.

"She's buried in the woods behind the house. Along with four other kids who were never reported as missing."

"What happened to them, babe?" Deke asked.

"They pissed off Mrs. Pierce, that's what happened." Cassie growled.

"Do you know where they're buried?" Sullivan asked.

"Yes, I know where the bodies are. That's one of the reasons she wants me back. She has to make sure I don't talk to the police."

"We need to get on this before she has a chance to move the bodies," Sullivan said.

"She can't," Cassie replied.

"What do you mean?" Deke asked. "Didn't she bury them?"

Cassie nodded, then grabbed Peaches' hand. "She did but I dug them up and reburied them where she wouldn't find them again. I couldn't leave them all alone out there. At least this way, they would be together."

"But you were so young when all this happened," Deke asked her as he felt stunned. "How could you do all that when you were a kid yourself?"

Cassie shrugged. "You just have to find a way to get it done. I did what I had to do."

"Mrs. Pierce never knew what Cassie did," Peaches spoke up again. "Once she buried the bodies, she never went back to them, she never checked on them. It was Cassie who got up at daybreak to make breakfast for everyone. Mrs. P always slept until noon. When one of the kids had a bad dream, it was Cassie who sat up comforting them."

"I'm not a saint," Cassie protested.

"No, you aren't but you are a very good person," Peaches countered. "All the kids except for Robbie, looked up to you. That was the reason she beat you so much. You had control where she didn't."

"This means you'll have to come back to Boston and show us where the bodies are," Sullivan stated.

Cassie shook her head. "I can give you a map, but I'm never going back. Even if you put that bitch in jail, my life is still in danger. The people associated with her are dangerous. I will never be free to simply live my life. I'll always have to watch my back."

"No baby, you won't," Deke spoke up. "We'll protect you, I'll protect you."

Cassie shook her head. "I can't allow you or your men to put their lives in danger for me." She cupped his cheeks with her hands around his face. "I don't want anyone to die for me."

"You aren't leaving here," Deke stated. "We won't let you go."

"I don't want to leave," Cassie said as she glanced at Peaches.

For a moment, neither said a word.

Then suddenly, Peaches bolted from her chair and ran to the kitchen crying.

Reva frowned and followed her.

~* * * *~

"What is it?" Reva asked the sobbing girl.

Peaches just cried harder.

Reva wrapped her arms around her shoulders and rocked her for a moment. "Are you okay hon?" Reva asked.

Peaches laid her head on the older woman's shoulder and replied,"No, but I will be. Cassie made sure of that."

"What are you talking about?"

"She'll make sure Lance Sullivan will find out where I came from," Peaches told Reva. "She always promised me she would do that. Find out who I was, I mean."

"She'll be there when he does that," Reva assured her.

"No she won't," Peaches whispered while hanging her head. "She's leaving soon and this time, she won't be back."

Reva's heart stopped as she stared at her. "How do you know?"

"I just do. I always know."

"You have to tell Deke," Reva told her.

Peaches shook her head. "It won't make any difference. He can't keep her here. She won't put anyone's life on the line. She doesn't think she's worth someone else's life."

"Well, she'd be wrong about that," Reva retorted. "These boys will protect her. They may belong to a motorcycle club but they are all good men."

"If Cassie doesn't want to be found, she won't be found," Peaches whispered with certainty in her tear filled eyes.

~****~

Cassie turned and stared at Lance Sullivan. "After you deal with the bitch, I want your promise that you will find out who Peaches belongs to. I want you to find her family and return her to them. She deserves that much consideration. She can still make something of her life."

Sullivan nodded. "I can do that."

"You'd better because if you don't, I will come after you," she assured him. "Even if it's from beyond the grave."

Deke wrapped his arms around her. "Baby, that bitch isn't ever going to touch you."

Cassie rested her forehead on his chest. Then she tipped her face up to his. "Will you promise me something?"

Deke nodded.

"Please make sure Peaches is okay when this is over. Help me keep my vow to her."

"You both will get through this," Deke vowed. "I promise you that."

Cassie patted his chest. "Thank you."

Before Deke could say anything, Wiley came to the door. "Boss, I think you need to see this."

CHAPTER NINE

Deke and Cassie went to the door.

Cassie gasped and Deke growled when they saw what was waiting for them.

In front of the locked gates stood three men in dark suits. Every three feet, along the fence on both sides of the men, stood soldiers. They were armed and had their weapons pointed at anyone and everyone standing inside the fence.

Cassie looked around, not one of the men inside the compound moved. Their hands were raised in the air. Most of the men wore frowns and the look in their eyes showed they were not happy.

Deke turned and glared at Sullivan. "What the fuck is going on here?"

Sullivan stood and began gathering the evidence Cassie had given him. "I had no choice but to call in the FBI who were associated with the case. When they knew the girls were here, they came along in case you wouldn't allow the girls to leave." He looked up at Deke. "I know this doesn't sit well with you. And it doesn't sit well with me either, but I need those girls back in Boston to answer questions. With their testimony, we have a chance to lock down one of the biggest child porn rings this country has ever had."

"I should fucking kill you where you stand," Deke whispered with a growl in his voice.

Sullivan nodded. "I know what you're feeling. I didn't want to bring them here either, but I had no choice. They want that ring busted up."

"What's going to happen to the girls, once the feds have what they want?" Gator asked Sullivan.

"They will go into witness protection," Sullivan stated.

"But you told me you'd find Peaches' family!" Cassie cried out.

"I'm sorry." Sullivan shrugged. "But it's better this way."

Cassie charged at Sullivan with her fingers curled like talons. "You bastard!"

Deke caught her around the waist and held her to him. "Don't. I'll find you and bring you home again," he whispered to her ear.

Zipper disappeared for a moment then when he returned, he had two denim vests in his hands. "Before you go, we'd like to present these to the girls."

Sullivan stared at the vests. They were made of simple blue jean material with the Satan's Spawn logo on the back. He shrugged. "I think it's okay. I mean I don't see anything wrong with it."

Zipper handed one vest to Peaches and carried the other vest over to Cassie. "Please wear these with pride and make sure you don't lose them."

Cassie stared at the man then his fingers lingered on hers for a moment after he handed her the vest. She narrowed her eyes and nodded as she said, "Thank you. I'll wear this with pride and always remember the men behind the patch."

Zipper grinned while Deke helped her don the garment.

Peaches wore hers as she and Sullivan joined them by the door.

Sullivan looked over at Deke. "I'm sorry things worked out this way. I know you're mad about this but think of the bigger picture. With their help, we can do so much more than anyone knew."

Deke growled low in his throat. "Watch your back, one day I'll be there to return the favor of stabbing you in it."

Cassie wrapped her arms around Deke's neck. "One last kiss, please."

Deke's mouth covered hers and when her lips parted his tongue delved into her mouth. Their kiss was hot, wet and heavy. Cassie felt the tingle of his possession all the way to her toes. When she pulled back, she had tears in her eyes. "That is what I'm going to miss the most," she whispered.

Deke watched as she turned to follow Peaches and Sullivan to the fence.

Gator was there to punch in the code that opened the gate. He waited until the three of them were outside the gate, then he punched in another code that closed the door.

Everyone watched as the soldiers backed away and began loading into the vans. When the doors closed behind Cassie, Peaches and Sullivan as well as the three men in suits, the vans backed out of the driveway.

Deke and the others stood and watched until the vans disappeared. Deke turned and slammed his fist into the wall, splitting the wood. "I'm gonna fucking kill that man. When I find the girls, I *will* kill him!"

"You don't have to even search for her boss," Zipper told him.

Deke snapped his head around and glared at him. "What the fuck are you talking about?"

"I know where the girls are going," Zipper replied as he smiled.

"What are you talking about, fool?" Gator growled as he joined Deke.

Zipper shrugged his shoulders. "I had those vests made with a very special reason in mind."

"Cut to the chase, Zipper," Deke ordered.

"I placed a tracking device in the collar of each vest," Zipper announced. "We can track where the girls are taken."

"And if we can track them, we can retrieve them and bring them back here," Deke whispered.

Gator placed his hand on Deke's shoulder. "We can't just ride into Boston and take the girls back. It's too dangerous."

Deke nodded. "I know. The Sinners aren't going to be happy we're there."

"Unless we can make it worth their while," Gator said.

Deke looked over at his friend and vice president. "What are you suggesting?"

Gator shrugged. "Hell...I don't know. There has to be something that fucker wants that we got."

Deke scoffed. "If there is, I don't know about it." He ran his fingers through his hair. "Iceman hasn't gotten his rep by being a man who's easy to talk to."

"No." Gator laughed. "The bastard is after his own name painted with fortune and glory."

"Maybe you can appeal to his better side?" Zipper suggested.

"He doesn't have a better side," Deke snapped. Even as he reached for his phone, his mind was racing with empty ideas. He tapped a number he rarely used.

"Who the fuck is this?" Iceman growled into the phone.

"Iceman, it's Deke Tory, President of Satan's Spawn in New York."

There was silence for a moment then Iceman spoke, "What the fuck does Satan's Spawn want with me?"

"I'm calling to ask if my men and I can come through your town on a rescue mission," Deke spoke with the upmost respect in his voice.

"Now, why would you and your men need to visit my city? Who are you gonna rescue?"

"The Feds and one Lance Sullivan who took my girlfriend from me," Deke informed him. "They claimed she was the only person who could bring Mrs. Eleonore Pierce down." He paused then asked, "Have you heard that name before?"

"Fuck yeah!" Iceman growled. "Been watching her for years. Do you know what she's mixed up in?"

"Yeah, I know what the bitch is doing."

"Can this girl bring her down?" Iceman sounded very interested in Deke's answer.

"Yeah..." Deke replied. "She can bring the bitch down."

"Then maybe, she's where she needs to be right now."

Deke took a deep breath and let it out. "I can't lose her," he admitted. "The Feds are putting them in Witsec as soon as the Pierce woman is taken down."

"Brother, I hate to help the Feds do any fucking thing but this would be a good happening. This Pierce woman is bad news. She peddles kids for Christ's sake."

"I know what she does," Deke growled. "You and I peddle pussy, so we could be considered just as bad."

"No, brother," Iceman corrected. "The pussy we peddle is of legal age. Kids under the age of ten, are not."

Deke exhaled. "I just need passage through the city. I want to find my girl and get the fuck out."

Iceman hesitated then admitted, "Now, is not really a great time."

"Why is that?"

"The ruling family is not happy."

"What the fuck does that mean?" Deke asked.

"The Vincinti family," Iceman explained. "Calderone Vincinti left last week to run down a clue to the whereabouts of his kid. He got back today and he's not happy. The city is on lockdown until he gets over his disappointment. Believe me brother, you don't want to be here right now."

"I have to be there," Deke replied. "I have to get my girl back." He ran his fingers through his hair again in frustration. "What's the story with this Vincinti anyway? He can't find his kid, so he holds an entire city hostage?"

"No my friend, it's deeper than that," Iceman explained. "Sixteen years ago, Louisa Vincinti was killed in a car accident, young Peaches disappeared and Calderone can't find any sign of her. It's driving him crazy."

"What did you call the girl?" Deke demanded.

"Her name was Peaches. Well, I guess it would be her nickname. I don't really know what her real name is."

"What is her father's name?" Deke asked, remembering something Cassie had once told him.

"Calderone Luca Vincinti."

"Fuck me!" Deke whispered. After a moment he asked, "Do you know how to contact this guy?"

Iceman was silent for about thirty seconds then he blurted out, "What the fuck do you want to contact him for? Are you fucking nuts?"

"No, I'm not." Deke chuckled. "What does his daughter look like?"

"Hell, I don't know."

Deke heard him move around for a moment then he came back on the phone. "I had an old info wanted poster hanging on the wall. It came out about the time the girl disappeared. It's got a color photo on it. The girl is blonde with long curly hair."

"Are her eyes gray?" Deke asked.

"How the hell did you know that?" Iceman exclaimed.

"I'll tell you when I get there," Deke stated. "Just call this guy and set up a meet. I promise you he won't be sorry and you can take the glory. I just want my girl back."

"If you're wrong, he'll hang us both," Iceman said in a low voice.

"I hope to hell I'm not wrong then." Deke ended the call and glanced at his men. "I found us a way in and maybe, just maybe found what Peaches has been searching for."

"Do you really think she belongs to the Vincinti's?" Gator asked.

"I guess we'll find out when we get to Boston."

"Let's hope you know what you're doing," Gator muttered.

Deke motioned to his men and said, "I want twenty five of you guys to ride with me. Gator will choose. The rest of you stay and protect home base. We ride in twenty minutes."

~*****~

Three hours and twenty minutes later, Deke and his men slowed and pulled into the wayside just outside the city. When he came to a stop, he faced Iceman and his men. He took off his sunglasses and reached out his hand to Iceman.

Iceman grasped it and they shook. "He wants to see us as soon as you get here."

Deke nodded.

"Is your info true?" he asked. "Do you know where his daughter is?"

"I think I do." Deke stared at him.

"Let's hope you do brother, otherwise he's gonna kill us both." Iceman started his bike engine and led the way.

Deke rode side by side with him and his men followed.

When they reached the warehouse district, Iceman raised his hand and curled his fingers into a fist.

Deke did the same.

The Satan's Spawn and Sinner bikers sat on their rides and watched as their leaders rode up to the warehouse alone. Everyone watched intensely as their bikes stopped beside the open door, they dismounted and walked inside.

As Iceman and Deke walked inside, they could see several armed men standing around. Their footsteps echoed as they made their way to the table where a single man sat.

Deke kept his eyes on him and he hoped this man was the one. As they got closer to the table, Deke caught his eyes.

The man had a cool but intense gaze. Like someone who was used to wielding power and taking charge.

Deke held out his hand.

Calderone hesitated then reached out.

As their hands met, Deke smiled. Hearing several ominous metallic clicks all around him, Deke let go of his hand and sat down. "I didn't come here to hurt you."

Calderone and Iceman sat down. "Why exactly are you here, Mr. Tory?"

"I'm going to reach into my pocket and bring out my cell phone," Deke informed him. "I'm telling you this, so your men don't shoot me."

Calderone nodded.

Deke brought out his phone and searched for a photo. As he slid the phone toward him, he spoke, "She has your eyes."

Calderone froze for a moment, then staring at Deke, he reached for the phone. He picked it up with shaky hands and studied the image on the small screen. When he saw her, his face paled by at least two shades. After all these years, he found himself staring into eyes he thought he'd never see again. "When was this photo taken?" he finally asked Deke.

"Three weeks ago, when a redheaded woman came to my clubhouse looking for her friend. I met the blonde for the first time seven weeks ago, when she came to work for me as a dancer. I had no idea who she was and neither did she."

Calderone frowned. "What do you mean?" He turned in his chair and stared into the shadows.

An older man with gray eyes came over and joined him. He took the phone and stared at the young woman in the photo. Turning his gaze to Deke, he introduced himself, "My name is Leon Vincinti, I'm Calderone's father and this young woman's grandfather."

Deke nodded to the older man.

"Tell us what you know," Leon ordered as he sat down beside his son.

"When I met Peaches—" he began.

"Her name is Kalliegh Paige Vincinti!" Leon snarled.

"Father, please, let the man tell his story," Calderone insisted.

"I do apologize." Deke held up his hands. "But she's only been called Peaches since she was five years old."

Leon looked over at Calderone and they both stared at Deke.

"How is that possible?" Leon asked.

"She was injured at that time. My girl Cassie thinks she was in a car accident. She was covered in small cuts and had a bump on her head. Anyway, she didn't speak for several months and when she started talking again, she called herself Peaches."

Calderone shook his head. "That fits her mother called her that. But her mother was killed in a car accident when Kalleigh was five. We never found any trace of my daughter...it was as if she just disappeared."

Deke's face tightened in anger. "No...she just didn't disappear. Your daughter was taken to a holding house, where she lived in fear for the next five years."

"What sort of holding house?" Calderone asked.

Deke leaned forward. "Gentlemen, I have a story to tell you. It ain't a very nice story but you need to hear it. It's about two little girls. Their names are Peaches and Cassie."

It took Deke a while to tell the story. As he spoke, he noticed a change come over every man standing in that room. His words shook them all.

When he finished, Calderone's hands were fisted with rage. "How did you know to call me?"

Deke stared at him. "Cassie told me of the day you came to visit. The girls were about eight years old when you knocked on the door."

Calderone frowned. "Whose door did I knock on?"

"Mrs. Eleonore Pierce."

Calderone paused as he thought about the name. Then he shook his head. "I have no idea who that is."

"I believe Cassie said you called her Janie."

Calderone and Leon froze.

Calderone paled and he slowly turned to stare at his father. When he turned back to Deke, he asked, "Kalliegh was there, in that house that day?"

Deke nodded. "Mrs. Pierce paid a beat cop who brought her there a couple of years before. Cassie told me that when someone came to the door, all the children had orders to hide."

Caldreone looked enraged. "I can't believe she would do this to me!"

Deke swallowed hard and spoke quietly, "The bitch was peddling kids at the time, she still is. Back then and now, she has people on her payroll that hid her activities. Cops, judges, social workers, they all were bought and paid for. She earned her money then and now, by selling somebody else's babies."

"Where is my daughter now?" Calderone demanded.

"She's with my girl. I called earlier to ask Iceman if I could come and get them. He told me I couldn't, that you had the city locked down, so I asked him to set up this meeting."

Calderone glanced at Iceman for a moment then turned to Deke. "Is she here in Boston?"

Deke nodded and explained, "She and Cassie are in federal custody, awaiting Mrs. Pierce's arrest. Cassie made Detective Sullivan promise to find Peaches' family. He made that promise knowing he would never keep it. After they testify, the Feds are placing both girls in witness protection. They probably won't see each other or family ever again."

Calderone tightened his fingers into fists. "That isn't going to happen. Can you find the girls and bring my daughter back to me?"

"Yes I can," Deke assured him.

Leon leaned forward and stared into Deke's face. "Name your price."

Deke's eyes narrowed and he stared back at the man. Then his lips curled into a sneer. "I want nothing from you or your son. Cassie made me promise if Sullivan didn't see through with his promise that I would."

"And you want nothing for your troubles?" Leon frowned.

"No I do not," Deke assured him. "I'm here for Cassie and her friendship with Peaches."

Leon turned to Iceman. "What about you? What do you expect to get out of this?"

"I expect to get respect," Iceman said quietly. "Respect for me and my club."

Leon stared at the two men then looked over at his son. "What is your wish?"

"I want her back with us," Calderone said. "I want my baby daughter back where she belongs."

Deke straightened in his chair. "Will you allow Iceman and I to go get her and bring her back here?"

Calderone stared at him for a moment, then nodded.

"We don't need or want your men with us," Deke warned. "In fact, I'll go with only two of my men and so will he. Please, I'm asking you and your men to stay behind."

"My daughter has been missing for sixteen years!" Calderone growled. "I want to see that she's safely home at last."

"I can understand that," Deke agreed. "Right now, she's completely safe. She has Cassie with her and believe me, when I tell you, Cassie will protect her. She's been doing a good job of it for sixteen years."

"What is going to happen to this Pierce woman?" Leon asked.

Deke's lips thinned. "She'll probably make a deal and not spend one day where she belongs. The Feds want information on the kiddie ring she's mixed up in." He shrugged, "They won't protect her for long and when I find her again, she'll pay for her mistakes."

"Is there evidence to convict her?" Leon asked.

Deke nodded. "Yeah, Cassie told me of a hidden room in the house. She claimed the evidence is there. I don't know if the Feds know about it yet."

Leon raised his hand to Calderone's shoulder and squeezed. "Let us worry about this Pierce woman. It will be our pleasure to teach her about right and wrong."

"Go get your woman and bring back my daughter," Calderone ordered.

Deke got to his feet along with Iceman. He nodded at Leon and Calderone, then he turned and walked back to his bike.

As he swung his leg over the tank Iceman growled, "You'd better know where they are or our lives are forfeit. "

Deke nodded. "Then we'd better go get them shouldn't we?"

They rode back to where their men were waiting. Deke looked over at Zipper and Zipper gave him a location. Deke took Wiley and Gator with him.

Iceman took two of his men along as he announced, "The rest of you have to stay here. We'll be back.

Zipper walked over to where Deke was and handed him an earpiece. "I can let you know what's going on with this. I have satellite vision on them as well as night vision. Right now, I see four men, two inside two outside. This is a middle income residence, nice and quiet. When you get close, let me know and I'll lead you in."

Deke fit the earpiece into his ear before he turned his stare on Iceman. "We don't kill tonight, wound maybe but no one dies."

Iceman nodded and passed the info to his men.

Then all six men took off, disappearing into the night.

CHAPTER TEN

Iceman led them to a fairly nice neighborhood. He pulled over in a parking lot of a church. When the others shut off their engines, he looked over at Deke. "The house your girls are in is about a block away. I didn't think you'd want to announce our arrival."

Deke nodded. He got off his bike and stretched his legs. He grabbed his weapon from the small of his back and checked the magazine. Glancing over at Gator and Wiley, he reminded them, "No killing. We don't want to go to jail. We go in, get the girls and get the hell out of there."

Gator, Wiley and the rest of the men nodded.

Deke turned to Iceman.

He smiled at Deke and shrugged. "It's your show."

Using the cover of darkness, they made their way to the house where Cassie and Peaches were being held. When he could see the house, he tapped the earpiece. "We're here Zipper."

Deke heard Zipper's voice, "The girls are in the back bedroom. There is one man on the southeast corner of the building. The other man is in the shadows of the garage. The two men inside are in the living room."

"Okay, we'll take care of it." Deke turned and whispered the info to the men standing there. "Iceman and I will go around the back and get the girls. You guys take care of the men inside and outside."

The men nodded and melted into the night.

Deke and Iceman waited for a few minutes then went around to the back of the house. When they got to the room the girls were in, Zipper let them know. Deke went to the window and peeked inside. Cassie was resting on one of the beds in the room. Peaches was on the other bed. Deke could see Peaches had been crying. He knocked softly on the glass.

Cassie's head popped up and she turned to stare at the glass. She got up and moved over to the window. When she saw Deke standing there, tears rolled down her face. Her hand reached for the lock then the window slid open. Peaches had joined her and Cassie whispered, "What are you doing here?"

Deke grinned. "I came to get you back."

Cassie slid her foot out the open window. Deke grabbed her and pulled her through. A moment later, Peaches followed her and together, all four of them headed for the neighbor's back yard. Deke pulled Cassie into his arms and hugged her close. Then his lips came down on hers and for a moment, that's all that mattered to either of them.

Iceman broke the silence with a cough and Deke turned his eyes to Peaches. He smiled. She grinned back.

By then Gator, Wiley and Iceman's two men joined them. "Let's get the fuck out of here before those boys wake up," Gator grumbled.

When they got back to the bikes, Cassie got on the back of Deke's bike and Iceman invited Peaches on his. When they roared off into the night, Deke could feel Cassie's arms tighten around his waist. Nothing ever felt this right, this good. He'd never invited a woman to ride bitch, never found one worthy of it. Now, he had his Spitfire and he wasn't going to let her go—ever.

When they arrived back at the warehouse, Gator, Wiley and the two Sinner's broke off and waited while Deke and Iceman went to the door. When they dismounted their bikes, Deke grabbed Cassie's hand and Cassie grabbed Peaches' hand. All four of them walked into the warehouse.

Calderone and Leon were standing there waiting for them.

Peaches stopped and stared at the two men.

Cassie noticed her friend's actions and stopped herself. Looking from Peaches to the two men, she narrowed her eyes at them. "Peaches, do you know them?"

Peaches looked a little lost. "I don't know. They seem familiar to me but not from anything recent, more of a memory."

"Kalleiegh, baby, is it really you?" Calderone whispered. Tears rolled down his cheeks.

Peaches stared at him then took a step forward. "Do I know you?"

"Oh baby girl, I hope so. Peaches, baby, please say you remember me."

Peaches paled and sweat beaded on her forehead. She raised her fingers to her temples as if to rub away a sudden pain. She stared at Calderone for a moment longer before her eyes went wide. "Daddy...?" she called out.

Calderone opened his arms and Peaches ran toward him.

He pulled her into an embrace and held her to him. "Oh baby, I thought you were lost to me forever. I have missed you so much."

Peaches rubbed her nose into his chest and tightened her arms around him. "Is this for real?" she whispered as she stared at him. "Are you really here?"

"I'm here baby girl," Calderone assured her.

"Do you remember me as well?" Leon begged gruffly.

Peaches turned her head and stared at him for a moment, then grinned. "Oh Poppy, how could I forget you?" She left the comfort of her father's arms and snuggled into Leon's embrace. He hugged her close.

Calderone's arms wrapped around both of them.

Cassie looked up at Deke and smiled. "This...my friend, has made the hell of our childhood worth every fucking minute," she whispered as she wrapped her arms around his waist.

"Josette," a voice in the shadows whispered urgently.

Cassie leaned around Deke and frowned. When the voice called to her a second time and she saw a hand gesture, she stepped away from Deke and closer to the shadow. "Do I know you?"

When she got closer, she could see his face and it was one she never thought she would see again. She sneered. "What the fuck do you want?"

"Please, you can't tell them who I am," he whispered to her.

Cassie turned her head to see Peaches talking softly with her father and grandfather. Before she could turn back, the man beside her had grabbed her upper arm and was pulling her further into the shadows. Cassie turned to him, "Take your hands off me. I don't like to be touched."

"I'll do more than touch you if you give me away." He hissed as he brushed his hair away from his head. It was worn a little on the longer side and the color had toned down from the bright red it was twenty years ago. Now, there was gray mixed into the red.

"Get your fucking hands off me," she called out a little louder.

"Shut the hell up, you stupid twit," he whispered.

He went to shake her but Cassie had had enough. "Let me go you slimy bastard!" she yelled as she stepped away.

He went to grab hold of her again and Cassie leaned to one side. Her foot struck out and the man crumpled to the floor. He gasped and held his chest. He grabbed at her ankle but Cassie stomped on his hand. Then her foot struck again and she kicked him in the face.

He groaned and his mouth began to bleed. He curled into a ball and closed his eyes. He felt more than saw Cassie lean closer. "I told you I don't like to be touched, you bastard."

Deke, Iceman and Calderone came up behind her. Deke reached out and stopped Calderone just when he would have pulled Cassie behind him. Calderone turned to glare but Deke shook his head. "She really hates to be touched."

When Cassie turned to them, Calderone asked, "How do you know my man Theo?"

Cassie snorted. "Is that what he calls himself now days? Theo?"

Calderone looked from Cassie to Theo then back to Cassie. "His name is Theo Bellini."

Cassie shook her head and turned her head to stare at the man on the floor. "His name is Flynn Reardon."

Deke gasped.

"How do you know this?" Calderone demanded.

Cassie turned to look at him. "Because this is the bastard that sold me to Mrs. Pierce. She gave him a couple hundred dollars and he turned his three year old daughter over to her. He walked away and didn't even look back."

Calderone snapped his fingers and two other men suddenly appeared. They dragged Flynn up from the floor.

When they had him on his feet, he raised his head to stare at his daughter. His eyes were filled with hate and he spat blood on the floor at her feet.

Calderone backhanded him.

Cassie narrowed her eyes at her father. "How many times did you visit that house, old man? How many kids did you supply her with?"

Flynn just shook his head. "Shut your fucking mouth girl. You don't know anything." Turning to Calderone, he wailed, "She's a fucking liar. I was never there!"

"Cassie?" a bewildered Peaches called out.

She stepped around her father and stared at her friend. Cassie shook her head and said, "Oh Peaches, I'm so sorry."

Peaches frowned and shook her head. "What are you sorry about?"

Cassie raised her hand and waved at her father.

Peaches turned her head and stared at the man in question. Her eyes went wide and she backed away.

"Peaches," Calderone asked, 'How do you know him?"

Peaches turned and stared at her father as tears ran down her face. She raised her hands to her temples and began to sob. "I remember now," she whispered. "It's like a bad dream but it must be true." She turned and stared at Flynn. "I remember his face, but he was dressed differently. He was wearing a dark uniform. I think."

Cassie nodded. "This is the piece of shit that carried Peaches up to the house. He pretended to be a cop. I couldn't see his face that day, he was turned away from me but I saw the back of his head. I saw his hair. It was the same color as my hair. I didn't know who he was at the time but I remember my father had the same color hair I did."

Calderone snapped his head back around and searched Flynn's face. He read the truth of her words. He reached out, grabbed Flynn's throat and tightened his grip. "I should kill you nice and slow."

Leon stepped up behind his son and grabbed his shoulders. "Cal, don't kill him yet. We need the information he has."

A muscle is Calderone's jaw twitched. He glanced at the men holding Flynn. "Take him to the playroom."

Flynn eye's got huge and he began to beg, "Please don't do this."

Cassie moved to Deke and felt his arms wrap around her. She cried silently.

"Oh Cassie," Peaches whispered. "I'm so sorry."

Cassie turned her head. She broke away from Deke and the two girls came together. "I'm so sorry Peaches. I knew he was a bastard for what he did to me but to do this to you?"

Peaches leaned back and frowned. "What do you mean? Why should you be sorry?"

Cassie shook her head. "When he brought you up to the house that day I heard him tell Mrs. Pierce that he had a hell of a time getting you. He told her he had to ram the car and he wasn't sure if your mother was still alive or not."

Calderone grabbed her by the arm and swung her around to face him.

Cassie narrowed her eyes at his action.

"Daddy, please let her go." Peaches whispered fearfully. "She doesn't like to be grabbed like that."

"Flynn is the man who killed my wife?" Calderone shouted. He ignored Peaches' warning.

Cassie tried to pull her arm free but his grip tightened.

"Cal, let her go," Leon ordered. "She won't tell us anything until you do."

Calderone pushed her away from him. "To hell with this and to hell with you!"

Cassie rubbed her upper arm and glared at him. Peaches took a step closer but Cassie didn't want her to close in. She took a step away. Then she turned to Leon. "In the Pierce house there is a den. Inside the den is a hutch. Pull open the right hand drawer and you'll find a small white button. Press it and the hutch will open. There is a secret room behind it. That's where you'll find record books and tons of cash. I hope to hell you find this woman and end her life. If anyone deserves it, she does. If you let her live, I will come back here and you won't like it if I do."

Peaches gasped and stepped back.

"Did you just threaten my life, little girl?" Leon asked.

Cassie shook her head. "No I would never hurt you. You belong to Peaches, but I will hurt your business."

Leon didn't say anything for a moment then nodded. "Yes, I can see that you mean business, young lady. I don't know what you think you can do to hurt us but feel free to try. I assure you we will deal with this woman and we will shut her down."

"I have your word on that?" Cassie asked.

Everyone in the room gasped.

Leon straightened his stance. "I don't know who you think you are woman but just this once, I'll overlook your brashness and give you my word."

Cassie nodded then smiled. "Thank you. I'll give you the benefit of doubt." She turned to Peaches and wrapped her arms around the other woman. "I'm so happy you're finally home and that you have someone to love you again."

Peaches had tears in her eyes. "I wish you had someone too."

Cassie shrugged. "That was over a long time ago."

Peaches smiled. "I think Deke wants that slot."

Cassie turned her head and gazed at the man in question. "Do you think?"

"Oh yeah, I think." Peaches grinned.

Cassie kept staring at the man in question as he stood at the door to the warehouse. "I'm afraid. Do you think I can trust him?"

"I think you have to try," Peaches whispered.

"Are you gonna be okay?" Cassie asked as she looked unsure.

Peaches glanced over at her father and grandfather.

They smiled back.

Peached nodded and replied, "I think I have a good shot."

Leon walked over to the two girls. He held out his hands out to Cassie. When she hesitated then put her hands in his, he raised them up to his lips. Gently kissing them he said, "Thank you for bringing our girl home again. We heard some of your story and what you girls went through. I marvel at your strength. I also want you to know if you ever need anything all you have to do is ask."

Cassie nodded. "Please take care of my girl. She needs you and her father."

Calderone wrapped his arms around his daughter. "I will always be here for her. Thank you for what you did for her."

Cassie nodded then turned to see Deke standing close. "Can we go home now?"

Deke smiled. "Hell yeah, we can go home."

"Will I ever see you again?" Peaches called out.

Cassie laughed. "When you least expect me, just turn around and I'll be there. I'll stop in from time to time to check on you. I love you, Peaches."

"Don't stay away too long." Peaches laughed.

Deke led her away.

~****~

Calderone, Leon, Peaches and Iceman watched them go.

Iceman turned and held out his hand to Leon. "It was a pleasure doing business with you."

Leon grasped his hand. "I'm glad to finally meet you. You asked for respect earlier tonight. I can honor that request."

Calderone and Peaches wandered away leaving Leon and Iceman to talk.

Calderone took his daughter back to the table and sat down beside her. He reached up and brushed her hair out of her face. "Are you really okay?" He sighed heavily. "I never thought I'd see you again. I have looked for you for a very long time."

"Oh, Daddy," Peaches exclaimed. "Cassie kept me safe! With her beside me, no one touched me. I owe her everything."

"I'll see that she's taken care of." Calderone nodded.

"If you knew her, you wouldn't say that." Peaches shook her head. "She doesn't want you to give her anything."

Calderone cocked his head at her and asked, "Then what? What does she want?"

"Nothing." Peaches smiled. "She would take nothing for getting me home. She did it because it's the right thing to do. She's got a sense of right and wrong that goes deep. She said she got it from her mother before she died."

Calderone gazed at his daughter in awe. "I was told her mother died when she was three."

"She did," Peaches explained. "Cassie used to tell me stories about her mom. Even if I knew they weren't true, I always listened. I didn't know how she could remember all that when I couldn't even remember my own name but she did."

Leon walked over to them. "What do you say, we go home? It's late and we all could use some sleep."

Calderone stood, then pulled Peaches up. The three of them walked to the back of the warehouse and got into a long black limo. It pulled away and disappeared into the night...Peaches finally got her life back.

CHAPTER ELEVEN

Deke threw his leg over his bike and waited for Cassie to climb on the back. *Where she belongs.* Deke fought the grin that threatened to show.

Gator grinned at her and revved his motor. "Glad to see you Spitfire." Gator nodded at her.

Cassie looked over at him. The name was something that surprised her. She then gave him a dazzling smile. She leaned forward and whispered into Deke's ear, "Can we stop somewhere for the night? I need some sleep. I'm wiped out."

Deke turned to look her over. "Are you all right?"

"It's just been some hellacious days I don't want to repeat." Cassie shook her head. "I'm just tired of all the bullshit." She wiped a tear from her cheek. "And I'm going to miss that girl."

Deke patted her hand and started his engine. She held on while he moved down the street. Almost at the outskirts of town, he pulled into the parking lot of a motel. Deke and most of the guys disappeared into the office. Gator and the others waited with her. A few minutes later, Deke came back and grabbed her hand. Leading the group, he found the door that matched his key card. He motioned to the next several doors for his guys to go to. Then he and Cassie went inside.

Cassie followed and flopped down on the bed. Groaning, she rolled over and closed her eyes.

Deke flicked the keycard with his finger then sat down beside her. "I need to ask you something."

Cassie opened her eyes and looked at him.

"Why did you go with Sullivan so easily this morning?" he asked.

Cassie stared at him then she replied, "He promised he would find Peaches' family. I had to give him one chance to keep his word. When he told me he had to put us both in witness protection after we testified, I knew he wouldn't keep his word. We were getting ready to leave when you guys showed up."

"Did you know who she belonged to?"

She shook her head. "No, but I knew where to find the evidence I needed to be sure."

"Where was the evidence?"

"In the secret room in the Pierce house."

"How did you know that for sure?"

"I've been in that room," Cassie explained. "I was too young to realize it the first time I was there. But I know more now."

"And if old lady Pierce caught you?" Deke growled. "What would happen then?"

Cassie shrugged. "She would have killed me, I suppose. Or she would have tried, but I'm not the scared little girl she once knew. I've learned to take care of myself."

"Why did you tell Leon where the room is?"

"I wanted someone to find it. I hadn't gotten the chance to tell Sullivan yet, but I wanted someone to know."

Deke reached out, grasped her face with his hands, and gazed into her eyes. He leaned over her and pressed his lips to hers. Cassie opened her mouth and groaned as his tongue slipped in. Deke's hands slipped under her shirt and he passed his fingers over her breasts. Squeezing them, he pushed her shirt up and uncovered her. Pulling the cups of her bra down, Deke moved his mouth down to suck on her nipple. "I missed you and this," he whispered close to her skin.

Cassie arched her back as his hand slipped down to her pants. He unbuttoned her jeans and his hand disappeared inside them.

She felt his fingers bury themselves deep inside her body. Cassie gasped and moaned. "And—I missed this..." Her words were breathless.

Deke buried his finger deep then added another and another. When he was thrusting three fingers deep inside her, he could feel her respond. His cock throbbed against his zipper. He pulled away and whispered, "I need to be inside you now."

Cassie pulled away and tugged her clothes off.

Deke joined her and settled himself between her legs. Without a word, he thrust his cock deep into her.

Cassie closed her eyes and moaned as thrust after thrust had her ready to explode. "I'm so close."

Deke ramped up the speed and hardness of his strokes. He felt the zing of his climax approaching and he thrust even faster. He felt her body tighten as he pulsed in her deep.

Cassie wrapped her legs around his waist and held on as Deke sank into her.

Deke finally rolled to her side. Wrapping his arms around her, he held her close. "I could get used to that," he whispered as he kissed her temple.

Cassie sighed and said, "I don't know how long we can be together. Sullivan and the Feds won't just let me go. Peaches will have her father to protect her, so they will more than likely come after me."

Deke leaned over her and gazed into her eyes. "They'd have to get through the entire club to get to you. We will protect you from them."

Cassie sighed. "I know you'll try but I don't want anyone dying for me. You guys mean the world to me and I don't want anyone hurt. At best, you all could go to jail."

"What are you going to do?" Deke felt his heart slow, then race up again.

"I don't know...I don't want to run again. I'm just tired of it all."

"Let's not worry about it tonight," Deke suggested. Reaching over, he clicked off the lamp, throwing the room into darkness. "Let's get some sleep."

Cassie snuggled in close to his warm, hard chest and closed her eyes. Drifting off to sleep, she felt safe again.

~*****~

It was still dark outside when Deke heard footsteps coming toward his door. Slipping out of bed, he pulled on his jeans and reached for his weapon. He heard the footsteps stop and a light tapping on his door. He crept close and listened. He heard his own name being whispered.

"Deke, it's Iceman. I need to talk to you."

Deke reached out and turned the knob. Very slowly, he opened the door a crack.

Iceman stood there and motioned for him to come out.

Deke slipped out of the room. Closing the door behind him, he walked down the hall a couple of steps. He then asked Iceman, "What can I do for you?"

"Your girl's information was dead on."

"Meaning?"

"Before we left tonight, Leon asked me to check out the house. He wanted me to bring the bitch back to him. Her and any evidence I could find." Iceman shook his head. "We hit the motherlode. I'm guessing he's going to use the information he found and either do the right thing and shut down this baby ring or take it over. If he takes it over, he's going to lose a lot of credibility. Nobody likes baby porn. I'd rather deal with legal women than kids. I also think if he doesn't shut it down, your girl will come back after him."

Deke grinned as she said, "She just might."

Iceman shook his head. "I ain't never seen anyone like her before. I can see why Gator calls her the Spitfire. You tell her if she don't want you anymore, she should come find me. I'll treat her like a queen."

"Not fucking likely." Deke growled.

Iceman held up his hands. "No offense man." He grinned as he shifted his feet and leaned against the wall. "On another note, thanks for including me in this rescue. I made another contact tonight and it never hurts to have that family behind you. I can still cut you in for a percentage."

Deke shook his head. "I don't want it. I told you that earlier. All I wanted was to get my girl back. You keep all the glory." He hesitated then asked, "I will ask for something you could give me."

"And what would that be?"

"Safe passage through your city when Cassie comes back to see Peaches."

"That's a no brainer, man." Iceman grinned at him. "If anything happens to her, I think old man Vincinti would crucify the person responsible."

"He just might," Deke agreed. "I haven't heard the whole story yet, but the girls have more secrets they need to tell."

Iceman shook his head. "Man, when you started telling their tale, I got sick to my stomach. I know some people are cruel but what those two girls went through, man."

"I'm worried about the badges," Deke told him. "Along with the Feds and what they'll do when they realize the girls are missing."

Iceman shrugged and said, "They can look all they want but if old man Vincinti doesn't want them to find Peaches, they won't find her.

"What about old lady Pierce?"

"I don't think you need to worry about that bitch either," Iceman hinted with a gleam in his cold blue eyes. "She took his baby girl and mistreated her. That won't go unnoticed in his world. In fact, I'd hate to be in her shoes right now. With the cops, she may have gotten a deal but with him?" He shrugged. "I don't think so. She'll be lucky to save her own skin."

"We'll be going back to New York tomorrow," Deke informed him.

Iceman held out his hand.

Deke grasped it.

"Safe travels man," Iceman said. "Keep the home fires burning and watch over that woman of yours, she's something special."

Deke nodded. "I will. Take care friend and if you need our help, don't hesitate to call." He watched as Iceman walked down the hall. Slipping back into his room, he noticed Cassie was still sleeping. Taking off his pants, he got back into bed.

"Did Iceman get the bitch?" Cassie whispered.

Deke felt his heart jerk. "I thought you were sleeping. Yeah, he got her and he took her to the Vincinti's."

"Let's hope he does the right thing." Cassie closed her eyes and drifted back to sleep.

~*****~

A few hours later, a knock rattled on the door.

Deke jumped up and looked around. At first, he didn't know where he was. The knock sounded again. He pulled his jeans on again and answered the door.

It was Gator and he looked pissed.

"What the hell?" Deke asked with a growl in his voice.

"She's gone, boss."

"Who? Who is gone?" Deke ran his fingers through his hair and glanced toward the bed. It was empty. His Cassie was gone. She'd left him during the night. He looked back at Gator. "How did you know?"

Gator pushed a letter into his hands. "She left this under my door."

Deke wandered back to the bed and sat down. He sighed as he gazed at the letter in his hand. Then he read it.

Gator, I'm sorry but I can't stay. I can't and won't put anyone's life in danger. Life is too precious to throw it away for someone else. I know Deke won't understand my decision, so please tell him I love him. And to give him up is killing me but I have to do this. I'll stay here for a while until I know Peaches is taken care of and maybe someday, I'll come back to him. Someday, when I know no one is looking for me. When no one remembers the name Josette Rearden. I hope he can forgive me.

Cassie

Deke crumbled the letter in his hand. He felt a burning in his eyes and a hole in his soul.

"What are you going to do?" Gator finally asked him.

"I'm gonna find her," Deke vowed.

Gator sucked in a deep breath. When he exhaled, he asked, "Are you sure you want to do that?"

Deke looked up at his second in command. "I can't do anything less. I need her."

Gator grinned. "I was hoping you would say that." He rubbed his hands together. "Let's find your spitfire woman and get the hell out of Dodge. I miss my Reva."

Deke threw on his shirt and checked his phone for messages. He didn't find any, so he called Iceman.

"Hello?" Iceman answered.

"Iceman, do you have the number for Calderone or Leon?"

"Why do you want to know?"

"Cassie left in the night. We stopped at a motel and she slipped away. She left a note saying she was going to stay here and watch over Peaches. I need to know where she might go. I need to find her."

Iceman sighed. "Damn...that girl is a bold one. Do you need some help looking for her?"

"No, I just need a number to call, so I can talk to Peaches."

Iceman gave him the number and when he called, Leon answered. He explained that he needed to talk to Peaches and that it was urgent. When Peaches got on the phone, Deke told her what happened.

She began to cry. "You have to find her."

"I will baby girl but I need your help," Deke insisted. "Where would she go? She said she wanted to watch over you until she knew you were going to be okay."

Peaches was weeping on the phone as she replied, "Okay, I know of a couple of places she might go. One place is a cave down by the water. Under the old McFlint's Fishery warehouse. We stayed there for a while. If she isn't there, she might be on the ridge above the city. There's a cave up there by a cell tower. Either place is isolated and she will be able to see you coming. Please let me know if you find her. I need to know she's safe."

"Peaches, I think you need to know something," Deke spoke quietly. "I love her and I think she loves me too. She left because she doesn't want anyone to get hurt on her behalf."

"I thought that might be her reason." Peaches sighed and said, "Sullivan and the Feds won't drop this thing. But my grandfather told me this morning he would take care of the police. They won't be coming after either of us, but Cassie doesn't know that."

"When I find her, I'll tell her that."

"I hope you can love her enough to get past her scars," Peaches told him. "Some of them you won't be able to see and they run deep."

"I can do that," Deke whispered. "All I ask is that she gives me a chance."

"When you find her, make her believe that. She needs someone who cares about her. She needs someone who will show her what love is all about. I think she needs you."

"I need her too," Deke admitted.

"Then you find her and never let her go," Peaches whispered.

"That's the plan, baby girl."

"Good luck," Peaches said before she hung up.

Deke ended the call and looked over at his second in command. "Take half the men and search the ridge above the city. There's a cave by the cell tower."

"Uh, Deke," Gator paused. "Iceman and his boys are waiting outside. I think they want to look for her too."

Deke got to his feet and went outside.

Iceman and twenty of his men were mounted on their bikes, waiting for him.

"This is not your business man," Deke stated to him.

"But it is my city," Iceman reminded him.

"All I want to do is find her and take her home. We won't be here longer than necessary."

Iceman shrugged. "I understand that, man. I just want to know she's okay."

Deke stared at him. His spitfire really drew people in. He knew this all too well. She was an amazing, courageous woman and he couldn't really hold it against the Prez of The Sinners. Finally, he nodded. "I have half my men under Gator, searching one area and I'm taking the rest with me to search another area. "

"My men can split up and go with you."

"Tell your men no one touches her," Deke insisted. "She doesn't like to be touched."

Iceman chuckled. "I remember very well. They all are too smart to wanna beatdown from her." His cool eyes twinkled with amusement. He turned to his men and announced, "Half of you go with his second in command, Gator. The other half come with Deke and me. No one touches the girl. Just try to talk her into letting you bring her back here. If you guys find her, she can ride with Gator."

Their engines roared to life and bike after bike tore out of the parking lot. There were a lot of bikers in these two clubs who were willing to do whatever they could to bring the Spawn's Spitfire back safely. They all knew her story and she had their solemn admiration.

Deke and Iceman were the last to leave. They took the lead and circled around the city to the water's edge. Parking their bikes in the warehouse parking lot, the men made their way to the water's edge and began searching for the cave Peaches spoke about.

"She worth all of this to you?" Iceman asked Deke.

"Yeah, she is," Deke told him. "She's come to mean a lot to me. My life would be pretty empty without her."

Iceman grinned. "I hope someday to meet someone like that."

"Boss, I think I found the cave," one of Iceman's men called out.

They both turned and saw the man pointing to a darkened spot nearby. Deke and Iceman rushed to it and when they got there, they peered into what looked like a cavern.

Deke looked around a bit and found a flashlight hidden beside the door. He leaned over, picked it up and was surprised to find that it worked. "Someone has been here." He glanced at Iceman.

He nodded. "Let's hope it's your girl."

Deke shone the light and it did little to disperse the darkness of the cavern ahead of them. Making their way inside, they both saw fresh footprints in the dirt.

Coming around a corner, they saw a camping area. In the middle of the floor was the makings of a small fire. A log had been dragged inside to sit on. A backpack leaned against the opposite wall and there were several other flashlights sitting in the dirt.

"How did you find me?" Cassie's voice asked from the darkness.

"Peaches told me about this place," Deke admitted. "How could you leave like that?"

"I told you I didn't want anyone to get hurt on my behalf," she said as she came out of the shadows.

Iceman paused, then said, "I'll meet you outside."

After he was gone, Deke pulled her to him. "I'm never letting you go," he whispered in her ear. "I love you girl, don't you know that?"

Cassie sighed. "How can you love something like me?"

Deke leaned back and stared at her. "What do you mean something like you?"

Tears were rolling down her cheeks. "People in my past tried their damndest to break me. They beat me, scarred me and carved me up. They tore chunks of flesh from my body and ripped my soul apart." Her voice was little more than a whisper. "How can anyone love that?"

"How can I not love you?" Deke asked. "You may be almost broken but you learned to mend yourself. You are the most honest person I've ever met. You are brave and kind hearted. Loyal to the bone. You cared for and about Peaches most of your life. You brought her home to her family when no one else would. You learned to take care of yourself and other kids like you when they would have been abused or worse. You stood up for them and took the beatings when it should have happened to someone else. Those kids didn't see you as broken, they saw you as their hero."

Cassie sniffed. "But I'm no hero."

"I'm no hero either, baby. I'm just a man who loves you. I need you in my life. You complete me in a way no other woman could or ever will."

Cassie turned and stared at him. "Really? You love me?"

Deke smiled. "I do love you."

"But I don't know love."

"Then I'll teach you," Deke assured her. "We can learn about love together."

Cassie trembled in his arms. "I want to learn. I want you to teach me but I'm scared."

"Of what?"

"I'm scared that I'll never be the person you want me to be."

Deke chuckled. "I only want you to be yourself. I'm not looking to change you. I love you for who you are right now."

"I've been alone for so long," Cassie whispered.

"So have I," Deke admitted. "I know about being alone. I also know about finding something better. I found you and I don't want to lose you. Baby, I can't let you go. I can't go back to being alone anymore. I need you." His arms tightened around her.

"I think I need you too." She paused, then said, "I think I have to tell you something."

"What?"

"When we make love I have a feeling you're holding back. I'm not sure what it is, but I can feel it."

Deke sighed and laid his head on hers. "I didn't want to scare you. Sometimes, my loving can get a little wild."

"Will you show me?" Cassie whispered. "I want so much to learn how to love you, but I can't if you hold that part of you back."

Deke kissed her temple. "Okay, I won't hold it back anymore. Come on baby girl, let's go home." He turned and led the way into the sunshine. "We've got a lot to explore." He squeezed her ass.

Cassie jumped a little and then she grinned at him.

Everyone was waiting for them in the parking lot.

Iceman smiled when he saw her and nodded at Deke. "Your men will meet you at the crossroads outside of town. Have a safe trip back."

Deke held out his hand. "Thank you."

Still grinning at him, Iceman shook his hand.

Cassie broke away from Deke and went over to Iceman. She leaned in close and gently kissed his cheek. "Thank you for helping my friend Peaches and me last night. I appreciate it greatly."

Iceman smiled. "You bet little Spitfire, it was my pleasure." Then he revved his engine and peeled out of the parking lot, followed by his men.

Cassie went over to Deke's bike and even though she was small in stature, she managed to swing her leg over the tank. "Come on boys," she called out. "Let's go home."

His men all halted and swung their startled gazes up to the petite spitfire of a woman, sitting on the Prez's bike. Then they did what she said

Deke shook his head and grinned as he joined her. He started his engine and rolled out of the parking lot.

Book #2

Revenge And Retribution

"A Sexy, Suspenseful Series, Full of Surprises!"

Just when Cassie thinks her past is over...someone comes looking for her. Someone she and everyone else thought was dead a long time ago. She has a man in her life and her dreams are coming true, so when Robbie comes after her she has more to lose than she ever had before. Except this time—she isn't alone. She has friends and family to help her fight against the darkness that threatens her.

Then she discovers yet another surprise—she has a sister...

Look For

Sin's Bastards MC

Sin's Next Gen

Bratva Blood Brothers Series

About K. J. Dahlen

Author of the bestselling, award winning Bratva Brothers and Satan Spawns MC Series...

I live in a small town (population 1,000) in Wisconsin. From my deck, I can see the Mississippi River on one side and the bluffs, where eagles live and nest on the other side. I live with my husband Dave and dog Bella. My two children are grown. I have two grandchildren and two great grandsons. I love to watch people and that has helped me with my writing. I often use people I watch as characters in my books and I always try to give my characters some of my own values and habits.

I love to create characters and put them in a troubling situation then sit back and let them do all the work. My characters surprise even me at times. At some point in the book, they take on a life of their own and the twists and turns they create becomes the story. Of all the stories I could write, I found I like mystery/thrillers the best. I like to keep my readers guessing until the very end of the book.

Join K.J. Dahlen's Reader Group[1]
Newsletter[2]

---

1. https://www.facebook.com/groups/1538834079503734/

2. https://confirmsubscription.com/h/j/C38BC78874901A2F

Don't miss out!

Visit the website below and you can sign up to receive emails whenever Kj Dahlen publishes a new book. There's no charge and no obligation.

https://books2read.com/r/B-A-OQCH-DSUV

BOOKS 2 READ

Connecting independent readers to independent writers.

Also by Kj Dahlen

Badass Women
Badass Women-Savaged Sous MC
Badass Women-Sin's Bastards
Badass Women#3 Brothers Of Chaos
Badass Women-Bratva Blood Brothers
Badass Women-Lost Sons MC
Badass Women VIM
Badass Women-Bratva New York

Bikers Of The Rio Grande
Rambler
Hunter
Sinner
Bearcat
Wizard
Raven
Taz
Thunder
Thunder & A Little Bit Of Lightning
Snowman & Eden

Born Of Desperation
Nitro
Pagan
Repo
Typhoon
Montana
Capone
Dixon

Bratva Blood Brothers
Yuri
Mikial
Barshan
Sazon
Roman
Brothers United
losif
Kosta
Nikoli
Nicky
Sergi
Misha
Timor
Felix
Kirill
Sasha
Maxim, A Bratva Christmas
A Bratva Christmas
Mikial-Father's Day

Valentines-Bratva
Sergi's Father's Day
Bratva Blood Brothers Thanksgiving

Bratva Born
Nubric
Koyla
Petrov
Minki
Dima
Catch
Bratva Women-Prequel-Bratva Born

Bratva Enforcers-Nomads
Viktor
Ivan
Adrik
Andrey
Grisha
Matvey

Bratva New Orleans
Bratva New Orleans#1
Bratva New Orleans#2
Bratva New Orleans
Bratva New Orleans#4

Bratva New York
Nikoli Bratva New York
Misha-New York
Nicky-New York
Felix-New York
Kirill Bratva New York
Sergi Bratva New York
Bratva New York
Christmas-Bratva New York
Crimson- Special Edition

Brothers At Arms MC
Zeus
Diabolus
Memphis
Grave Digger
Click
Captain

Cajun Kings
Cajun King
Fat Tuesday
Born In Fahyuh
Crazy As Hell
Sweet Rascal
I Don't Give A Damn

Cajun Queens
Cajun Queens
Cajun Queens#2
Cajun Queens #3
Cajun Queens #4
Cajun Queens #5
Cajun Queens#6

Crimson Tide MC
Tracker
Boomer
Cyrus
Clovis
Vance
Tether
Crimson Tide MC

Destiny Meets Fate
Destiny Meets Fate
Destiny Meets Fate#2
Destiny Meets Fate#3
Destiny Meets Fate
Destiny Meets Fate
Destiny Meets Fate #6
Destiny Meets Fate Set

Devil's Advocates MC
Jackal
Beast
Wolf
Apollo
Shade
Tank
Shadow Hunter
Devil's Advocates Series Set

Devil's Own MC
Stormy

Devils Trifecta MC
Gage
Joker
Sledge
Devil's Trifecta MC Set

Fire And Ice
Fire And Ice
The Flame
Invincible
Supernatural
Incandescent
Extraordinary

Ghost Riders MC
Pepper
Phantom
Dax
Venom
Heathen
NiteStalker

Hell's Bloodhounds MC
Barron
Leonid

Hell's Fire Riders
A Hell's Fire Christmas

Hell's Fire Riders MC
Pappy's Shadow
Betrayed
Trigger The Storm
Shay
Legend
Birth Of Hells Fire Rider
Trudy

Kings Of Wrath MC
Pride
Candyman
Rage
Scar
Romeo
Cosmos
Kings Of Wrath
Kings Of Wrath Christmas

Lords Of Hell MC
Mayhem
Brutus
Bear
Stone
Tag
Svante

Lost Sons MC
Creed's Return
Jack
Tate
Harry
Silas
Daniel
Silas & Midge
Come Home-Lost Sons MC
Lost Sons MC

Louisiana Heat
Ajax
Fireball
Stinger
Moon
Racer
Player
LA Heat Series

Malverde
Malverde
Malverde 2
Malverde 3

Masters Of Mayhem MC
Rance
Bull
Korbel
Rocker
Nova
Ram

Misfits Of Whiskey Bend
Misfits Of Whiskey Bend

New Blood-Savaged Souls MC

Arrow

Beau

Hayes

Runner

Acer

Duke

New Blood Savaged Souls-Boxed Set

Payback

Ghoster

Phantom Fury MC

Shilo

Bullet

Princes Of Hell MC

Talon

Rogue

Falcon

Condor

Princes Of Hell MC Set

Reunion Series

Reunion
Silk & Bones Reunion
Hell's Fire Riders Reunion
Yuri Bratva Blood Brothers Reunion
Rogue's Of Hell MC-Reunion
Reunion Sin's Bastards MC- Next Generation

Rivers Foundation
Cade

Rogues Of Hell MC
Titan
Kota
Brute
Nash
Wanderer
Hawkins
Rogues Of Hell MC Set
Rogues Christmas

Rogues Of Hell MC Trilogy
Cash

Rogues Trilogy
Wilder

San Francisco Steel
Slammer
Shotgun
Grinder
Mammoth
Booker
Spider
Texas

Satan's Spawn MC
Spawn & Spitfire
Revenge and Retribution
Babies & Bastards

Savaged Souls MC
Boone
Gunner
Jett
Cobra
Thor
Gypsy
Grizzly
Moose
Skeeter

Shades of Shay Trilogy

Shades Of Shay
Shades Of Shay
Shades Of Shay

Shadow Warriors
Blue

Silver Warriors
The Quest
The Ride
The Brothers
The Game
The Fall
The Race
Coming Home
Silver Warriors-Boxed Set
Silver Warriors Halloween

Sinners MC
Hawk
Pony
Prosper
Saber
Rebel
Buzz
Sinners- Boxed Set

Sinners Of Boston
V-Sins & Sinners
Atlas
Echo
Cuffs
Ringo
Dak

Sin's Bastards MC
Silk & Bones
Karma's Bite
No Regrets
Hell's Fury
Lies & Liars
Stone Cold
Sin's Bastards Christmas
Leon
Mountain
Peaches & Iceman
Girl's Night
Sin's Bastards Mother's Day
Bane Returns
Christmas With The Sin's
Deacon
Reva

Sin's Bastards Next Generation
Raine

Chance
Gambler
Bowie
Judge
Byron
Hound
Dante
Iceman
The Kids
Wiley
Calderone
Sin's Bastards MC Next Generation Boxed Set #1
Vincinti Women
Sin's Bastards Next Generation Boxed Set #2
Jericho's Christmas

Soldiers Of Hades MC
Cottonmouth
Python
GTO
Lightning
Whiskey
Spirit
Cobra's New Year
Soldiers Of Hades Christmas

Sons Of Ireland
Sons of Ireland-Boston#1
Sons Of Ireland

Stone Cold Bitches MC
Calypso
Widowmaker
Aqua Velvet
Medusa
Razor
Ruby Red
Stone Cold Bitches MC Set

Swamp Patriots
Swamp Patriots

Tennessee Breeds
Breed
Greer
Monster
Crow
Maverick
Cowboy
Blade
Tennessee Breeds Set

The Boondocks
Mad Dog
Stroker

Vengeance Is Mine
Bane
Damon
Bane's Shadow
Cane
The Priest
Kill Me Twice
Kill Me Again
Lionheart
Lancelot
Galahad
PenDragon
Excaliber
Palamedes
Calegis
Escalades
Theo
Hell's Vengeance
Archangel
Butterfly
Blue Eyes
Dante's Inferno
Conquest
Apocalypse
Poison
Into The Black
White Noise
Absolute
Doom
Faith
VIM Set

Bane's Infinity
Valiant
VIM #2

VIM Redux
VIM Redux

Vincintis
The Vincintis
The Vincintis#2
The Vincintis#3
The Vincintis#4

WarLords MC
Truman
King
Jack- WarLords
Deuce
Joker
Traven
Giving Thanks-Warlord MC

Whiskey Bend MC Series
Lucifer's Woman
Demon's Stand
At All Costs

Out Of The Shadows
Jinx
Shadow
Cooper
Bender
Saint
Whiskey Bend MC Set
Christmas In Whiskey Bend
Whiskey Bend Easter
Misfits Christmas

Wings Of Fire MC
Maze
Tabor
Sayer
Hellion

Standalone
Hell's Fire MC Series Set
Satan's Spawn & Sin's Bastards Collection
A Life For Luke
Chasing Eve
Saving Sebastian
Shadows Of The Past
Never Forget Me
The Cartouche
A Wrath Is Born
The New Brotherhood
Slade
Zipper

Carson
San Francisco Steel MC Set
Return To Yuri
Patriot
Badass Women-Boxed Set
King Of Pain Vol.#1
King Of Pain Vol.#2
Shades Of Shay Collection
Cobra's Christmas
Cajun Queens Boxed Set